ENDORSEME

T0169432

Nine ½ Months is an odyssey of the soul. Gracie displays Godly bravery and courage as she struggles with the decision to abort or keep her child. Bonnie has the creative ability to capture a story that wrestles with faith and future.

Dr. Rev. Joe Kirkendall
(Bonnie's Pastor) New Life Manitou

Sometimes single moms need to make dangerous decisions. You'll be stunned at the process Gracie goes through to make sense of all the hard options in front of her. Come along with her on this perilous journey—and see God at work in ways you may have never imagined.

Doug Schmidt
The Prayer of Revenge: Forgiveness in the Face of Injustice

Nine ½ Months is rich with humility and openness. Prestel captures her memories with detail and dialogue, inviting readers into her perspective with the power of story instead of confronting them with an explanation. Her observations are like those found in the novels of Kent Haruf, and her total honesty reminds me of the memoirs of Anne Lamott.

John Sloan
President, Creative Director
John Sloan LLC

Nine 1/2 Months

Nine 1/2 MONTHS

A NOVEL

BONNIE PRESTEL

NEW YORK

LONDON • NASHVILLE • MELBOURNE • VANCOUVER

Nine 1/2 Months

A Novel

© 2020 Bonnie Prestel

Published in New York, New York, by Morgan James Publishing. Morgan James is a trademark of Morgan James, LLC. www.MorganJamesPublishing.com

ISBN 9781642793826 paperback
ISBN 9781642793833 eBook
Library of Congress Control Number: 2018914101

Cover Design by:
Megan Dillon
megan@creativeninjadesigns.com

Interior Design by:
Chris Treccani
www.3dogcreative.net

Illustration by:
Freepik.com

Morgan James is a proud partner of Habitat for Humanity Peninsula and Greater Williamsburg. Partners in building since 2006.

Get involved today! Visit
MorganJamesPublishing.com/giving-back

For God's two precious gifts—Kayla and Johanna

And for Tim—my forever love

Thank you for believing in me and my story—

and for being the hero in our fairy tale.

ACKNOWLEDGMENTS

My deepest thanks and love to my dad and mom—Jim and Phyllis. Thank you for your unconditional love and patience. For driving to the Bronx to bring me and Kayla home. Dad, for staying up all night to watch the U-Haul. For pacing the floors with your first granddaughter. For your strength and joyful spirit.

Mom, thank you for never giving up on me. For supporting me even when we disagreed. For taking the girls shopping for school clothes, baking cookies, and reading stories. For being the thread that keeps our family connected.

Sincere thanks to Kay for living your life with passion and adventure, which inspires me. Thank you Mike, for your deep soul and true friendship. For Mary, thank you for your contagious laughter that brings us all joy and hope. Thank you Kerrie, for loving Mary.

I want to acknowledge and thank my two new daughters for being in my life and sharing their dad. Christine, your faith and courage are inspiring. Alli, your strength and ambition are admirable. Thanks for being my "actress."

I will be forever grateful to Father Charlie Brown. For speaking the truth that Sunday about the sanctity of life. For opening your door to me when I was in distress. For the train tickets and ride home from the hospital. For accepting me in love.

I want to thank Ted and Audrey Becket for speaking prophetic words over me and mentoring me in my walk as a new believer. For believing God would use me as His poster child for single mothers.

Thank you, Marlene Bagnull, founder of Write His Answer Ministries. Your writers' conferences equipped me, comforted me, and gave me the courage to write His answer.

Thank you Meredith Sloan for editing the first draft of my story. Your talent and wisdom helped shape the manuscript into what it is today. I also want to thank John Sloan. Your kind, honest critique of my manuscript gave me the confidence that maybe I did have a gift and I could publish my stories.

I'd like to thank my editor and friend Doug Schmidt. For taking me under your wing as an editor at David C. Cook and for editing this first manuscript with precision and care.

Thank you, Robert Benson. You captivated me with your words and gentle spirit during the Glorieta writers' conference. You made me want to be a writer.

My heartfelt thanks to Ann Fallon, my sweetest friend, who encouraged me to keep writing every time I wanted to give up my dream.

And a sincere thanks to Deb Hudson for her never-ending prayers and spiritual support through the battles of life.

Thank you, Misha Byrom, for your faithful friendship. For standing by me as I brought my daughter into the world and for being there for all her big life events.

I am grateful for Terry Whalin, acquisitions editor for Morgan James Publishing, for taking the time to talk to me and believing in my story.

Thank you to the creative team at Morgan James Publishing for their work in creating this beautiful book.

In memory and great gratitude for my steadfast friend Pat Couchman. You stood by me during the most difficult time in my life. You now reside in heaven but live in my heart until we meet again.

CHAPTER 1

The metal table was cold. Stubby hairs stood up on my bare legs. My thighs, moist with sweat, stuck to the transparent paper. I waited, dangling my legs over the side, hoping the doctor would enter soon.

I wanted to get this over with and get back to my life—if I could find a life. Eight weeks earlier I had been lounging on the beach, letting the waves rock me to sleep. Lee snuck up behind me, waking me with a salty kiss. He just got in from the surf. His face was flushed as he described the huge waves that day. His passion for surfing and zest for life were what attracted me to him.

But now he was gone.

Eight-foot waves didn't scare him, but an eight-pound baby sent him running.

The heavy footsteps coming down the hall reeled my thoughts back to reality. *He's here,* I thought. *Finally.* I adjusted my position on the table, ripping the soaked paper as my legs shifted. He entered in silence. It took him a few moments to acknowledge me. I searched his face trying to find some comfort. In a soft voice he told me to lie down. Silently I obeyed.

I felt a cold substance plop on my belly. The doctor moved a scope around my tummy like he was searching for coins on an abandoned beach. Suddenly he stopped. "There it is," he said. "That's your baby's heartbeat."

I lay there paralyzed, staring at the ceiling. I couldn't look at the screen. The sounds reminded me of the waves hitting the shore. I wondered if Lee was surfing today.

"Do you want to see your baby?" the doctor asked.

"O–okay," I stammered.

It sure didn't look like a baby, just a messy inkblot. Kind of like my life. I wanted it removed. Gone.

The doctor turned in his swivel chair and then left the room. Thirty seconds later he was back with a silky square of paper. "Here's a picture of your baby, just eight weeks old," he said, handing me the inkblot image. I stared at it through a haze of tears.

"Do you still want to go through with it?" he asked.

I couldn't speak.

"You know," he said, "I'd much rather bring babies into the world. . .but if you still want to. . . ."

"No, no!" I cried. "I don't. I can't. I need to go."

Smiling, he said, "All right. Get dressed, and we'll talk. I'll need to see you again in two weeks."

I don't remember getting dressed and leaving the office. The next thing I knew, I was on the corner of 82nd and Park trying to hail a cab. "Taxi!" I shouted. "Taxi!" I saw many yellow cabs, but not one of them had its *Available* light lit. *Just my luck*, I thought. I ran up a block and tried again. "Taxi!" A yellow cab swerved over two lanes to pick me up. I flung open the door and slid in the backseat.

"Where to?" the raspy voice asked.

"The Bronx, 205th and Mosholu Parkway."

"That's quite a journey. Want me to take East River Drive?"

"I don't care. Just get me home."

I sat in the backseat, still holding my slippery photo.

"What ya got?" the driver asked.

Oh, great, I thought. *A chatty cabby.*

"A picture," I said, glaring at her.

"Of what?" she pressed.

I wanted her to shut up, but she persisted, "Of what?"

"A baby!" I exclaimed.

Ignoring my disdain, she said, "Congratulations! You're gonna be a mommy."

"Oh, yeah, yippy," I said sarcastically.

"When's your due date?"

"May 10," I said.

"Hey, maybe she'll be born on Mother's Day."

"Great."

"Is it your first?"

"Yep."

"Is Daddy excited?"

"Nope. Daddy's gone."

That last answer finally shut her up.

I closed my eyes, trying to escape my world. Fifteen minutes later her voice broke the silence. "You know, you're going to be a great mom. Once you hold that baby in your arms you'll be hooked. I envy you. This is the best gift you could ever receive. You sure are blessed."

My eyes opened to the words *gift* and *blessed. Was she high? A young single girl having a baby alone in New York City. Yeah, I'm blessed all right. More like cursed.*

"Trust me. You don't believe it now, but this baby will be the best thing that ever happened to you." The cabby smiled a knowing grin.

I leaned forward, peering into the front seat. Next to her ID photo plastered to the dash was a larger photograph of a girl in her late teens, maybe early twenties. Above the photo hung a cross-stitched purple cross. "Who's that?" I asked.

Beaming, she said, "That's my baby, Brie. She's the love of my life. She just graduated and got a scholarship to Vanguard. God is good."

I glanced at her left hand gripping the wheel. No ring. *Did I dare ask?*

"So how long have *you* been married?

"Oh, I'm not," she answered without emotion.

I just stared at her. Finally I asked, "Why not?"

She glanced back. "I told you already." Her head tilted toward the photo and the cross. "They're my family. The loves of my life. I have all I need."

I sat back and slumped down in the vinyl seat. Her words echoed in my head. *All I need, all I need.* Those words had the same power as the waves, lulling me to slumber. Surrendering, I closed my eyes.

CHAPTER 2

What seemed like five minutes later was really fifty. The cabby's voice startled me. "We're here, love. Wake up." Dazed that fifty minutes had passed, I glanced at the meter and offered the fare with the last money I had. Thirty-five dollars plus tip. I had two ones left.

"Here you go," I said as I leaned forward handing her the wad of money.

"Keep it," she said. "I don't want your money. Buy something nice for that baby of yours."

"But. . . ," I protested. "You drove me all the way to the Bronx. Are you sure?"

"Keep it," she said. "And get out of my cab. I need another fare to get me back to the city. I'm lost up here."

I sat still, not willing to believe her generosity. I handed her the money again.

"Really, take it."

"I told you to get out already," she blurted back.

"Okay, okay, have it your way." I stumbled on the curb getting out and slammed the door. She drove away as fast as she had picked me up. I stared in unbelief as her cab number lit up like a firefly: 7777.

I turned and started walking toward my battered brick building. Kids were playing ball on the sidewalk, and an old man was sitting across the street playing solitaire on a park bench. It was an unusually hot September day. The air smelled like baked beans and sauerkraut. Miss O'Leary was cooking again.

I climbed up the stairs of the five-story walk-up. As I reached the second floor, the smell of that German food only got stronger. It never used to bother me before, but now the scent made me feel like I had a bad hangover. I bent over trying to hold in my insides. I paused on the landing. *One more floor to go*, I thought. *I can make it.*

Sweat covered my forehead as I neared the top of the stairs. I turned left and walked down the hall to the apartment I shared with Michelle, my friend from high school. As I got closer, it looked like the door was already open.

That's weird, I thought. *Michelle should be at work. Why would the door be open?* I kept walking, but taking slower, cautious steps. I peered inside before entering. "Michelle!" I called. No answer. I looked down and saw the metal rod lying on the floor. Normally it snuggled into a groove near the doorknob under the two dead bolts. Just one more piece of protection. But our three-lock metal system appeared to have failed. As I stared at the rod, it began to roll toward the kitchen.

"Michelle!" I called louder. Still no answer.

I looked both ways as if crossing the street and then walked toward my bedroom. I held the doorknob for a few seconds, took a deep breath and opened the door. Everything was just as I left it. Futon on the floor. Blankets a mess. Shoes in the corner. I blew out a sigh of relief and turned back toward the kitchen. It was so quiet. No TV, no sounds. I placed each foot in front of the other, heading across the hall to Michelle's room. A speck of black crossed my peripheral vision. A roach. A big one. More like the water bugs that lived in my room. He scurried across the floor and disappeared through a crack in the wall.

I brought my gaze back to my destination. Taking another deep breath, I took a bigger step, careful not to creak the floorboards.

Like the blast of a stereo, loud male voices broke my concentration. They were coming from down the hall. As the men got closer their voices were stronger and more urgent. I paused

to listen. I stood frozen, left foot in front of the right, waiting for a signal that it was safe to move. I inhaled and mustered the courage to take a step when a large man appeared inside my front door. I screamed and grabbed a spatula from the kitchen counter for protection. Startled by my scream, the man stopped and looked at me like I was some crazy woman.

"What are you doing here?" he said in a low angry voice.

"Shouldn't I be asking you that question?" I barked. I stared at him, spatula raised in my right hand. "I live here!" I shouted as loud as I could so the neighbors would hear.

His eyebrows raised, and he said, "Okay, calm down, miss. Calm down. I'm Officer Kelly. Everything's going to be all right. Can I get your name?"

"Gracie. Grace O'Connor."

Just then my roommate, Michelle, came huffing up the stairs and entered through our wide-open door.

"Michelle!" I exclaimed. "What's going on? Are you okay?" She looked frazzled standing there in her white robe and matching slippers.

"Someone broke into the apartment today just after you left for the city," she said.

"What? You were home? I thought you went to work."

"I didn't go in today. I called in sick. I was lying in bed half asleep when I heard the door slam open. I thought it was you, forgetting something. I yelled your name, but there was no answer. So I lay there a minute and then called for help. I heard some noise in the living room and got up. Holding the phone in one hand and my bat in the other, I opened the door to the living room in slow motion."

"Oh, my gosh! Someone was in here?"

"Yeah, and he found my purse, dumped it out, took my money and ran. My stuff was all over the floor, lipstick in the hall, my keys on the couch."

"Thank God you're okay. He didn't go after you?"

"I don't think he knew I was in there. He broke the door and was in and out in minutes," she said.

I sat down. My nausea was back. Officer Kelly had been examining the place. He was taking pictures of the door. He walked over and said, "I need to get a statement from the one who was in the bedroom." He eyed Michelle up and down, her robe now half open and the whites of her thighs exposed.

"Michelle," I said.

Sounding more annoyed than afraid, Michelle said, "Sure, I'll give you a report."

I snuck away to the bathroom, fell to my knees, and proceeded to lose my breakfast. When nothing was left to heave, I collapsed on the cold tile floor, cradled my head in my hands, and wept.

How could I bring a baby into this horrible place? What am I going to do?

Michelle pounded on the bathroom door. "Hey, you okay in there? I need to shower and then catch the 4:20," she said.

I dried my eyes with my sleeve, splashed water on my face, and opened the bathroom door. With a fake smile I said, "Sure, I'm fine."

Michelle just stared at me like she was trying to figure out what happened. Then her gaze shifted from my face to my belly. "How'd it go?" she asked, "Did it hurt?"

"No. . .it didn't."

"Well, that's good. They must've given you some good drugs," she said, grinning. "I'm glad it's over with." She combed through her bobbed hair.

I looked back at her. "Well, it's not over yet."

"What do you mean?" she asked. Her hand stopped combing. "Did you chicken out?"

"No, it's not like that," I protested. "I just couldn't do it." Remembering the shiny photo, I searched my pockets trying to find it. "I have a picture, Michelle. A picture of the baby. It really is alive, you know. I heard the heartbeat and everything. I just couldn't kill it."

She looked at me. "You're crazy," she said. "How are you going to take care of a baby? You can barely take care of yourself."

I couldn't say anything. She was right.

Michelle stepped back to grab a towel from the closet. A black water bug scurried out from under the cabinet.

"Those nasty bugs!" she yelled. "Can you kill the roach?" She slammed the door and cranked the shower on full blast.

Now we had a big gap between the frame and the front door, right above the second dead bolt. I bent down to peek through it. You could see the stairs through the cracked wood. I walked back into the kitchen to get a drink. Nothing but stale beer and old Chinese food in the fridge. I filled a glass with cloudy water. After waiting for the sediment to settle, I took a drink and crinkled my nose. The pipes started to clank as the shower turned off. Michelle would be out soon. I couldn't face her again. I grabbed my bag and slipped out the cracked door.

I headed south on the Parkway then turned right on Clancey and headed toward 204th Street. I walked past the laundromat where women were sorting socks in between chasing toddlers. The air was hot and sticky. In the corner pub I could see bare-chested men sweating on bar stools. I kept walking. Chubby women in tight sundresses strolled the sidewalks pushing strollers with half-naked babies. *Would that be my life?*

"No," I told myself. "Remember, you're not married. You'll never be a stay-at-home mom, pushing babies in the sun."

I turned back to watch the women in the sundresses cooing at their babies. And for a second I envied them. They had someone coming home for dinner. Someone to share the burden. I doubted they even thought of their little ones as burdens. Just the same, they were not alone.

I had no one friendly coming home for dinner. Michelle was mad. My parents were two thousand miles away. No way could I tell them and keep breathing. I turned and headed back to the corner pub to erase the disapproving faces from my mind.

"Hey, lassie, what can I pour ya?" asked Danny, the young bartender who looked like Harrison Ford's younger brother.

"A cold one, from the tap," I sighed.

"So what brings you in on this sweltering Tuesday?" he asked. "Playing hooky today, are we?"

His grin melted me into the plastic-covered stool. No way was I having this baby. *I'll find another way,* I thought. I chugged my beer. It tasted too good.

"Just taking a personal day," I said.

"Ohh." He grinned. "Otherwise known as playin' hooky." He winked at me as he walked away to serve a bloke hollering for his whiskey at the other end of the bar.

I gulped down the last bitter sip. I felt a little dizzy. Danny came back and leaned on the bar to get a closer look at me. "Hey, darlin, you look a little pale. You all right?"

It was all I could do to sit still while my empty stomach churned in beer. "I think it's the heat making me queasy."

"Ohh. I know what *you* need. A little hair from the dog that bit ya. What kind of dog got ya, darlin?"

Danny mixed the most potent hangover cures. Michelle and I had sampled a few after long nights of too much fun playing pool and listening to bands at Patty's. The pub was named after its owner, Patty Clancy, a good old Irishman. He had died four years earlier and left the busy bar to his three sons: Patty (the second), Danny, and Mattie (short for Matthew). Good Catholic boys. Just like my Lee. But Patty was a lawyer in the city, and Mattie couldn't be bothered to work before five o'clock. So it was left to Danny to run the pub, day and night. He didn't mind. It was good money, and in those days he needed money. The year before he had gotten his girlfriend pregnant, and they had a quickie wedding at St.

Mary's down the street. His little boy looked just like him—the same twinkly emerald eyes that teased all the girls. Danny was one of the good ones.

"Oh, no, no. No dog last night. I was a good girl. Home in bed by ten."

He looked at me suspiciously. "I bet you were. Hey, have you seen the latest?" he asked as he pulled out his wallet to retrieve the newest picture of his son, also named Patty, after his grandfather.

"No, let me see!" I said, reaching to grab the photo out of his calloused hand.

"Settle down, missy. I'll get it," he said. Like any proud papa, he pulled it out of the plastic protective cover and handed it to me. I stared at the little guy. He was definitely a Clancy boy. His green eyes danced and looked right into my eyes. And then I lost it. Started blubbering all over the picture, tears falling into my beer like some bad country song.

"Darlin, I know he looks like his grandpa, but he's not that bad." Danny tried to be funny.

It didn't work. I laid my head on the sticky wooden bar and sobbed without shame.

He handed me about twenty tissues to mop up the mess. I finally stopped long enough to blow my nose. The guy at the other end just stared at me and ordered another whiskey. Danny told the guy to hold on; he'd had enough anyway.

"I'm sorry," I said between blows.

"No apologies needed. Just tell me what I can do, darlin'."

I just shook my head. "Nothing. . .there's nothing. I just can't."

"Can't? Can't what, darlin'? Talk to me," pleaded Danny.

But I couldn't talk. All I could do was sob into the whiskey-stained bar.

CHAPTER 3

Sixteen weeks.

That's all the time I had left to decide if I was going to terminate this pregnancy. It sounded like an eternity when I thought of being pregnant—but when I thought of being a mom it was definitely not enough time.

I was no teenager—just celebrated my twenty-fifth birthday. Motherhood sounded so old. I wasn't ready. Michelle was right. I could barely take care of myself. How was I going to manage a baby? I thought about what the cab driver said to me: "You're gonna be a great mom." What did she know? How could she say that without even knowing me?

What was a *great mom*, anyway?

I slept through my alarm. The staccato beeps tried to interrupt my dream, but I was too far off to notice. I slapped the snooze button and rolled over. Ten minutes later the machine broke the silence, beckoning me to life. I used my forearms to push myself upright on the stiff futon. I sat in a fog, glancing at the clock. If I waited long enough, I would miss Michelle. I sat in silence holding my breath, straining to hear Michelle's heels clicking back and forth on the wooden floors. The only sound I heard was the sizzling wheeze from the radiator. The air grew colder each day, and mornings were the worst. I exhaled in relief as the radiator blew out a burst of hot air. The damp heat gave me the strength to lift my heavy body to my feet. I shuffled into the bathroom and squinted in the dim light. A note was taped to the oval mirror. Scribbled blue ink read, "Going to PA for the weekend. Taking the train after work. See ya, M."

I ripped the paper off the mirror, crumpled it and threw it in the hallway. It was Friday. Michelle and I always went to happy hour in the city after work on Fridays. We usually ended the night playing pool at Patty's down the street. We'd been practicing all summer and were darn good. Guys lined up their quarters on the rail to play us.

Those days were over.

I stared into my closet, trying to find something to wear. I pulled on my navy skirt, but the zipper would not zip up all the way. I got it as high as I could and then slid the skirt around my belly so the zipper was in front. I reached into my jewelry box fumbling around to find a safety pin. Underneath a long strand of fake pearls I found a piece of folded blue paper. Scribbled in black was a phone number. It was Lee's.

I remembered a day at the beginning of summer. I had taken the train to Long Beach on the first beach day of the season. I packed a lunch, found a good book, and slung my folding lawn chair over my arm. I walked briskly to the train, full of anticipation for the day ahead. A long lazy Sunday soaking in the sun. The water was probably still cold, but I didn't care. It was eighty-five degrees outside, and I was ready to shed my winter skin.

I snatched a window seat and settled in for the hour-long train ride out to the island. To my left sat other eager beachgoers armed with sunscreen and a small cooler. Two teenage girls sat behind me, playing a card game to pass the time.

I opened my book to read, but my mind would not stay on the page. I daydreamed about the smell of the ocean water, the sound the waves make when they hit the shore. I imagined tall, tanned surfers with beautiful bodies playing frisbee in the sand. Maybe today I would meet "the one." I would be lounging in my chair, half reading and half asleep. He would be playing catch with his other surfer buddies. One of them would overthrow the football, and it would land next to me, just barely missing my head. He would run with long lean strides to my rescue as I leaned over to grab the ball. Like a giddy girl I would toss it to him, throwing back my long raven curls. Our eyes would meet. Our lips widen into mischievous smiles. He would squat down displaying quads of steel.

His tan skin glistening in the sun, holding back the muscles in his chest, he would lean over. "You okay, beautiful?"

I'd smile, hesitating to answer, and then with one smooth exhale I'd whisper the syllables of my name like a song.

He would take my hand. "Tell me more."

Playing it cool, I would pause and ask him what he wanted to know.

With a smile in his eyes he would ask me my plans for the day and invite me to meet him at Tony's for oysters.

Of course I would say yes, to his delight.

He would squeeze my hand before standing up to his full six foot four frame and walk backward down the beach, blowing me a kiss in the salty air. I would swing my legs over my chair and stretch in the sand, leaning in his direction and waving with a casual shake of my hand.

I would swim in the waves and brown my body in the sun. A quick nap would give me energy for the date ahead.

As the sun began its descent toward the water, I would slip into my red sundress and strappy sandals. Taking my time, I would walk to the marina, arriving just a little late. He would recognize me from a distance and jump off his board, jogging toward me.

Finally we would stand face-to-face. He would take my hand and lead me inside Tony's, carefully guiding my high-heeled steps. A table would be reserved for us in the corner, away from the ruckus of the surf crowd. Steamed mussels and raw oysters would be waiting, along with two mugs of cold beer. He would pull out my chair and offer me my napkin. A true gentleman. As he sat, his eyes would never stray as he stared into mine. I would be the center of his world, not only at this first dinner, but always.

The rest of the daydream was standard stuff. A beautiful wedding on the beach, followed by a honeymoon in Paris, moving into a bungalow in the Hamptons and driving matching BMWs. The perfect life with the perfect man.

The neon numbers on the clock brought me back to reality. I had to run if I was going to make the 8:10 into the city.

"Miss, your ticket, please." The irritated voice of the conductor startled me. I searched my bag for my transit ticket, but it was not there.

"Hold on," I said. "I know it is here somewhere."

The conductor shifted his weight. "Miss, I need your ticket, now."

I emptied my pockets and my bag. In my frustration my book slid off my lap, and the ticket fell out on the brown matted floor. I forgot I'd been using it as a bookmark.

"Thank goodness!" I said out loud. Smiling, I waved it in front of his face. "Here it is! I found it!"

He punched it in silence, making no eye contact, and walked on to the next section. I sat back in my seat, closing my eyes, eager to return to my dream world, but the mood was broken. *He didn't have to be so rude,* I thought, almost out loud. I wished Bryan was working today. He was always friendly and polite. He would have let it go and gotten me next time. I hadn't seen Bryan in days. I think Sheila said he worked nights now. I would call her later. Or ring her, as she would say.

"Next stop Long Beach!" yelled the rude conductor. My stop, finally. I grabbed my book, bag, and chair and prepared to exit the train. The sun was beaming, beckoning me to come. I was eager to make my claim on the beach. So many people were there that day. Exiting the platform was like shopping at Bloomies on a Saturday. It was a sea of bright-colored beach chairs and coolers everywhere. I tried to get down the stairs as quickly as I could, to get out in front of the crowd and get a head start on the boardwalk. Prime beach spots were hard to find, and I was not willing to lose mine.

Hustling in front of me was a family of four. Dad speed-walked, holding Junior on his shoulders. Mom unfolded an umbrella stroller in record time and was wheeling her little girl in a hurry. I made a move to pass the foursome. Without warning the little girl dropped her doll, and Mom stopped on a dime. I stopped short, almost falling right over the stroller. I saw the baby crying, reaching her hands out to her fallen doll.

I could stop, turn around, and grab the doll for her—or I could keep going to claim my spot on the beach. I hesitated. I didn't even know this child, but I resented her. She was whining and screaming. It was annoying me. *Let her mom get the doll*, I thought. But something tugged at my heart and made me turn back to snag the ratty doll. I gave it to her, and her crying immediately stopped. The mom thanked me and quickly continued on to catch up with her husband. I readjusted my chair and plodded on. The crowd had already passed me up. *Babies are a pain in the butt*, I thought. *They mess up everything.*

I took the final step off the boardwalk, and my foot hit the sand. I stopped to slide off my flip-flops. The sand wasn't too hot. I wanted to feel every grain between my freshly painted toes. It felt so warm and soft, each step massaging my feet. Every muscle in my body began to relax. My irritation over the little girl in the stroller melted away. I had made it. I stopped halfway down the beach to scan for a spot. To my left, farthest from the water, sat families with small kids. I wanted to avoid that area. Down the beach, close to the water, teenagers lay in the sand giggling in groups. Not there either.

Then I spotted it. Five feet in front of the lifeguard stand was the perfect spot. Far away from the screaming kids and close to the fresh foamy water. I glued my eyes to the open spot and plowed straight ahead, navigating around beach blankets and bodies. Out of the corner of my eye I spotted a skinny blonde heading in the same direction. *Oh, no, you don't,* I said to myself as I leaped over a cooler and threw my beach bag, landing right in the open sand. *Yes, I made it.* I planted my chair and settled in for my day at the beach.

The sun's rays were straight overhead. It had to be noon. I rolled over to brown my backside. I bunched up my coverup and tucked it under my head, making a pillow. The heat from the rays and the beat of the waves coming in and going back out to sea rocked me to sleep.

The next sound I heard was the lifeguard's voice yelling through a megaphone, "Out of the water!" He was directing his command at a group of teenagers. I lifted my heavy head and squinted my eyes to see what was going on. The beach had thinned out, now only spots of people here and there. The waves sounded angry and loud. The tide was inching its way in, as if to say, "Move on out, time to go, the beach is all mine now."

Had I slept through the afternoon? I pushed up on my forearms, wincing in pain as my back arched. I felt like a pop tart, hot and toasty.

Again the lifeguard shouted, "Out of the water, man o' wars!" I pushed up to all fours and rotated my body in my sagging chair. Heat radiated from my back and shoulders. Gingerly I put on my white terry coverup dress and pulled my hair back into a high ponytail. I drenched my lips in gloss and swiped my lashes with a dab of fresh mascara. The day at the beach was coming to an end, but the night had just begun.

Tony's was only a half-mile up the beach. I dragged my chair in the sand and carried my sandals in my hand. I walked close to the water, letting the waves greet me as they came in with power hitting my bare legs. The sun was getting closer to the water and setting low in the pink and blue sky. I stopped to stare at the horizon. The beauty calmed my spirit, and my cares felt a million miles away. It was the perfect day, and I hoped the night would bring the perfect romance.

Rachel told me she would meet me at seven. She had to work on a Saturday and was taking a late train out from the city. She was the marketing assistant for a high-powered public relations firm, and she rarely got Saturdays off. She had a PR event on Roosevelt Island. My arms were bare and brown. I wasn't wearing a watch and had no idea what time it was. By the looks of the sun, it had to be getting close to seven. I could see Tony's just ahead. Butterflies jumped in my belly as I anticipated meeting Rachel and her friends. Especially her friend Lee. He was a surfer she had met weeks ago, and she wanted to set us up. The sun-bleached wooden shack was worn and old, but the white and blue Christmas lights wrapped around the deck blinked as a beacon of light. I dropped my chair next to the sidewall lined with surfboards and bicycles. I hid behind a row of boards to slip into a pair of Levi cutoffs that showed off my bronzed legs. With care, I removed my cotton coverup and stuffed it into my bag. I adjusted my top, tied a halter around my neck, tightened my ponytail, and walked into Tony's with feigned confidence.

Stomach in, shoulders back. The words of my mother echoed in my head. Conscious of every step, I felt as if everyone was looking at me. A group of bare-chested guys surrounded the first round table covered in clamshells and beer bottles. They hooted as I passed by. I kept my eyes focused straight ahead, searching the crowd for Rachel. I loved and hated the unsolicited attention from the boys. I felt pretty and ashamed at the same time.

Neil Young was screeching out "Heart of Gold" through the speakers, and people were huddled together around the wide wooden bar. I spotted Rachel. She wore a red strapless sundress, and her wispy hair skimmed her bare shoulders. She was talking to some guy in a wetsuit. I gently pushed my way through the crowd catching my bag on the back of a barstool.

"Hey, babe, where you going so fast? Sit a while." He patted his bare muscled thigh as an invitation to sit. He was kind of cute, curly blonde hair, nice teeth. But I wasn't interested.

"Love to, but I'm meeting someone," I said with a half-smile.

"Your loss." He grinned.

I unhitched my bag and kept moving toward Rachel. She was laughing and sipping her cocktail from a thin straw. She glanced up, and our eyes met.

"Gracie!" she yelled, as if I had been lost at sea for days. She lunged forward and embraced me with the drink still held high in one hand, almost spilling it on my head. "I can't believe you made it! I never thought you would come alone. There are so many people you have to meet." She started with the hunk with whom she was flirting. "This is Jeremy. He's a broker for an investment firm in the city." She slid her hand down his arm as she introduced him, like he was for sale on the home shopping network.

"Nice," I said. "Nice to meet you." He smiled and gave me a wink.

"Grace works at Walter T. Stedman. She's in broadcast traffic." Jeremy smiled and nodded his head. She grabbed my hand and pulled me away. "Isn't he hot?" she asked.

"Yeah, but does he talk?"

Rachel laughed. "He's shy, that's all. There're more people I want you to meet." She led me to a table full of people doing shots. One by one she rattled off their names. "And there's Lee. Remember that guy I told you about?"

Remember? He was all I could think about all day. I played it cool. "Oh, yeah," I said and turned toward him. He was cute. A little shorter than she had described. At first I was reluctant to meet him. He was her ex. They had only dated a few times, and she swore she did not sleep with him. But I was leery. It felt like getting someone's hand-me-down. But when I saw his smile I didn't care.

"Come on—let me introduce you two. I told him all about you," she said.

"What did you say?"

"Don't worry, only the good stuff."

"That's what I'm worried about."

"It's cool. He just wants to have fun. No pressure."

Slowly I allowed my head to turn back in his direction. He was cute. Short crewcut, dirty blond, and eyes as green as the sea. He caught me checking him out and flashed a shy smile. He was too good looking to resist. He stood against a table, his wet suit peeled down to his waist. His bronzed calves bulged under the black spandex. His chest, clean and smooth, was strong and proud. Definitely a surfer's body.

"Quit staring at him and go say hi," said Rachel.

"No! I don't even know him," I said.

"Do you think you'll get to know him standing over here like a Barbie doll?"

Rachel grabbed my hand and pulled me through the crowd across the room to meet surfer boy.

"Hey, Leeee," she said in her most flirtatious voice. She winked at me. "This is my friend, Grace, who I told you about."

He looked at me, top to bottom.

"Hi" was the only word I could say.

"Hi," said Lee with an approving smile. "Glad you finally made it out to the island."

"Me too." I smiled back.

"You need a drink?"

"Sure, a sea breeze."

"Hey, Todd, a sea breeze for my new friend."

He turned back to meet my eyes and grinned.

My heart fluttered.

CHAPTER 4

pulled my mind back to reality as I ran to the train, hoping not to miss the 8:10 again. The safety pin holding my navy skirt together had popped open, and the pin was poking my tummy. I wondered if the baby could feel it. *How stupid,* I said to myself. *Of course he can't.*

He.

That was the first time I referred to the baby as a specific gender. The thought of carrying a baby boy inside of me scared me straight. I knew nothing about boys.

The platform was now in sight. I could hear the sound of the engine approaching the station. I lengthened my gait and jumped up on the first step taking the rest two at a time. I'd been late for work every day this week. I had one more chance to make it on time. The ad agency I worked for was in Midtown, 46th and Madison. Once I departed the Metro train at Grand Central Station, it was a short walk uptown.

The train pulled in at 8:42. I had eighteen minutes to trek uptown and make it on time. I pushed my way through the swarms of people haphazardly making their way through Grand Central. I exited at 42nd Street and weaved through the line of taxis parked on the curb. I crossed the street and walked to my favorite Korean deli. Jake was behind the counter, serving the pack of people standing in a huddle in their khaki trenches and black shoes.

Jake glanced up and caught my eye. He knew my lack of time management as well as he knew me, and he yelled past the people, "Hey, beautiful, regular today?"

Embarrassed and elated, I nodded yes with a smile. And then added, "But no bagel."

"Got it, gorgeous," he answered without missing a beat of fulfilling the coffee orders in front of me. When our hands finally met, I exchanged my cash for the hot paper cup and mumbled a quick "Thank you."

He stared at me a little longer than usual with his piercing jet eyes. Kind of half smiling, he said, "You look more beautiful than usual today, gorgeous." Afraid he would discover my secret, I thanked him and slid back through the crowd out the door to 46th Street.

Three minutes to go as I punched the elevator button. The bells rang, and the doors slid open. I stepped in, letting out a heavy sigh and taking a sip of my hot coffee. As the steaming liquid ran down my throat to my belly, a nauseated feeling overtook me. The coffee didn't taste good at all today. The bells dinged again, and the doors slid open on the third floor. Two men stepped off, and a woman in three-inch heels stepped inside. I still had eighteen floors to go, and it was already nine o'clock. My efforts were wasted.

The harder I tried, the more I failed.

Finally the doors opened to the twenty-first floor—the offices of Walter T. Stedman. I loved the hustle and bustle of this agency. The creative department was my favorite. Jason and Scott worked in that department. I'd pop in later to visit. For now I made a beeline for my cubicle, praying that Wendy was away from her desk. 9:07. Late again.

Wendy's office was empty, and I slid into my chair. In two seconds I kicked off my running shoes and slid on my black pumps. I punched the return key on my keyboard so my screen would wake up from its sleep. The happy face appeared, and then my desktop magically filled with documents.

I checked my voice mail but got distracted by the high-heeled steps clicking down the hall. Wendy. I glanced at my screen, pretending to be engrossed in a document. She sauntered by, glanced at me and then at her watch. Shaking her head in disapproval, she passed me in silence and entered her office.

I felt her disdain, and I couldn't quell my bitterness. If I lived in a penthouse apartment on Park Avenue, I'd be on time too. But, no, I had to schlep in from the Bronx. It wasn't fair. My heart was so full of guilt and condemnation and envy I could not focus on my work. I got up to go visit the boys down the hall and get a new cup of coffee.

When I walked by Jason's cube he was shooting a nerf ball through an orange plastic hoop. "Hey, girl, think fast," he said as he tossed the squishy blue ball at my head. I caught it, barely. "Nice catch," he said.

"Working hard, I see," I teased him.

"Yeah, we're brainstorming for the new Miller campaign. Storyboards are due Tuesday," he said.

"Who's the AE on the job?" I asked.

"John, the slave driver," he said. "Nothing can please that guy."

"Yeah, I know the feeling. Nothing is ever good enough for that one. I don't even know why I try," I said.

"She's riding you again?" asked Jason.

"Yeah, the same old story," I said.

"Well, maybe if you'd get to work on time—"

"Shut up!" I cut him off in mid-sentence and threw the ball at his head. Jason grabbed the ball with his long skinny arm, yanking it out of the air.

"I'm just razzing you. Lighten up. Why are you so touchy these days?" he asked.

I slumped down and sat on the corner of his desk. I crossed my arms and hung my head. Gazing at my scuffed black pumps, I slipped my feet in and out of my shoes, stalling. Jason stopped playing with the ball and waited for me to speak. He knew I wasn't telling him something.

"What's up?" he asked, gently nudging my elbow. "What's going on with you? You're not your usual self. Where's that smile and the giggle I love to make fun of?"

He was trying to get me to laugh. To crack. Spill the beans. I wanted to tell him but didn't know how.

"Jason?" I said his name like a question.

"Yeah, that be me."

"Jason, can I tell you something?"

"Sure, you can tell me anything. You know that," he said.

I lifted my gaze up from my feet and looked him in the eye. "Jason. . . ."

"Just say it, girl."

"Okay," I said. "Jason, I'm pregnant. I'm like twelve weeks already."

"Woman, you're having a baby?" He looked at me, not in disgust, but with care and tenderness in his eyes.

"Well, I don't know. I mean I wasn't, you know, I wasn't planning to keep it," I said quite casually.

"Oh. Ohhh," he said and looked at his computer screen filled with dancing bubbles.

Words poured out of my mouth so fast I couldn't take a breath. "But I couldn't. I couldn't go through with it. It had a heartbeat and everything. I mean, how can you do something that will stop a beating heart? I just couldn't. I can't. Even if everyone on the planet thinks it is just a lump of tissue. . .some mass hanging out in my uterus. Formless, lifeless. But I heard it. It was real. A tiny thumping, little tiny heartbeat. It's alive in there, Jason. And I don't know what to do.

"It's living in there, and I don't want it living in there, but it is, and I can't get rid of it. I can't stop the beating."

Finally I stopped for a breath and used every ounce of strength I had to delay my tears.

Jason looked at me. He stood up, leaned toward me, and wrapped his skinny frame around my big body.

I felt the warmth and care in his embrace. I let my tears flow freely as he held me, and I sobbed into his chest.

CHAPTER 5

thought about Jason on the train ride home to the Bronx. He was so sweet. He cared—I hadn't counted on that. We'd developed a friendship over the two years we worked together. Even though I was in traffic and he was a part of the creative department, we got to know each other playing softball on the company team. I envied his position at the agency. That was where I wanted to be, writing jingles and slogans, designing storyboards and creating. But I was stuck in traffic. I thought it would be a foot in the door when I was hired.

During my interview the HR manager scanned my linen resume and looked at me confused. "Are you sure you want traffic? What about an account executive position or perhaps media?"

If I had had some self-confidence, maybe I would have considered her offer—but my insecure self settled for traffic. Most of my friends worked in other departments, and I thought that if I hung around them long enough I could be one of them. I joined the softball team and visited the corporate store—which was code for the company bar. Two floors up I could sit on a high stool, gaze through the glass windows looking down in the atrium, and indulge in cold beers and goldfish crackers.

I met Jason playing softball. We played against other agencies in town and then, win or lose, went out to party after the game.

Jason was a stand-up comedian on the weekends. He would entertain us pre- and post-game. He was shorter than I was and had a wiry body. He was fast and could run the bases like a pro. His sandy hair was messy, wild, and always trying to escape from under his baseball cap. The first day we met was in the field. We had an instant connection. Not romantic, but almost as if we'd been best friends for a long time. Gazing out the train window I smiled, thinking of Jason in his baseball pants with his skinny legs and stupid grin. I was glad he was my friend.

That's the way Lee and I started out—friends. After that initial meeting I would take the Long Island railroad almost every weekend to hang out with him on the beach. We always met at Tony's after he surfed all day with his buddies. The first night he shared surfing stories, and we laughed and danced on the deck. I quickly forgot Rachel had gone out with him first. Every Sunday night I would hesitate to leave and barely make the last train back into the city.

I saw Lee almost every weekend. The relationship was carefree and fun, and we were mostly party buddies. He didn't even kiss me until my fifth visit. I was beginning to wonder if anything would ever happen. But all of that changed one Saturday night. I spent the day lying in the sun listening to the waves as I flipped through magazines. Lee got up at the first ray of light and rode his bike down to the shore with his friend Mike. Mike was married with three kids, and sometimes his son Kenny would come with them. They all looked so good in their wet suits, skin glistening, muscles bulging, and strong arms hugging their waxed boards under their arms.

I loved to watch Lee run into the waves with his stocky body. He would jump high, board in his hands, and almost coast over the wake. Ten seconds later he'd be up on his board, arms wide, riding all the way in to the shore. He was as beautiful as a dancer on Broadway. I tried it a couple of times, but my clumsiness prevented me from conquering ripples, much less waves. I always slid off my board before I got to a squat. Then I'd wrestle my way out of the wave, pummeled by the force that threw me back to shore. My gift was lounging in a chair browning my body and watching the waves carry the boys out to sea.

Lee lived for it. Even when the waves got higher than eight feet, he paddled out to meet them. He was fearless. At least in the water.

That Saturday night we planned on going to a party after our day in the sun. I was excited to get out and socialize. Lee didn't have a car. He worked construction September through May and used a company truck. Come May, he shed his boots for a board and rode a beat up ten-speed. Long Beach was a small town so he got everywhere he needed to go by the power of his strong legs. We walked to the party. It was beginning to get dark, and Lee grabbed my hand. I felt like we were getting closer and hoped tonight he would finally kiss me.

George answered the door and welcomed us into his home. It was a faded blue and looked more like a shack than a house.

"Hi, I'm George." He reached out his long, scarred arm to shake my hand.

"Hi, I'm Gracie," I said.

He smiled. "I know. Come in. . .grab a bottle."

Lee grabbed two beers for us, and we found seats on a long bench outside on the back porch.

George looked old, late 50s. Maybe it was the damage the sun had done over the years. He still surfed every day. On his upper left arm was a band of ink. I tilted my head trying to make out his tattoo. The body art was written in some sort of script, and I couldn't make it out. He caught me staring and grinning, left his station at the gigantic gas grill to come near me so I could get a closer look. This was what it said: *"Therefore, if anyone is in Christ, he is a new creation: the old has gone, the new has come."* The words wrapped around his bicep, and a red cross anchored the phrase to his skin. I just stared, trying to comprehend. I had never seen a Bible verse written on skin. The only place I had read one was in the paper missalettes in church. I squinted as I read the small script. George proudly recited it in an authoritative voice, emphasizing the words "new creation." He beamed with joy.

I did not understand what it meant to be "in" Christ. Or the "new creation" part. I believed in God and knew Christ died on the cross for my sins, but I felt separate from Him. I was far away—definitely not in Him. The tattoo didn't seem to faze Lee a bit. He took a gulp of beer. Like me, he was raised Catholic but had not felt the hard wood of a pew in quite some time. We had that in common. I felt a pang of guilt about not going to church more—but I did not feel worthy. If I entered the doors now, the priest would surely see my sin and make me do thousands of Hail Marys to atone for them.

Two more couples joined us on the back deck, diverting my attention. A dark-haired girl, with large round hips, walked by. She gave me a quick glance and then said hi to Lee. It appeared they knew each other. She came with a guy, but he disappeared into the garage the minute they arrived. A lot of people kept entering and leaving the garage, which was on the property next door. George tried to ignore it, but I could tell it bothered him. It made me wonder what was in there.

Lee was talking motorcycles with one of the guys, so I went to satisfy my curiosity. I jumped down off the deck and crossed the yard, heading to the two-car garage on the corner. I heard guitar music and followed the sound. With care I turned the knob to the side door and pushed it open a crack to sneak a peek before fully committing. A group of guys and two girls were sitting inside on the cement floor. They passed around a thin, white, paper cigarette, taking long inhales before handing it off to the next person. The smell made me feel nauseous, so I closed the door, hoping no one had noticed my peeping. They were all too stoned to notice.

I walked back to the deck to find Lee. The bench was empty. I looked around, appearing lost. *Where did he go?* I wandered through the house looking for my date. Panic surfaced for a second, thinking he had left me alone.

I stood in silence, trying to breathe deep. Then George stepped into the hall and startled me. "Hey, sweetie, want a burger? Fresh off the grill."

"Where is Lee?"

"I'm not sure. Check down the hall."

"Thanks," I said, heading down the long hallway, peeking into rooms as I passed. The house was long and narrow like the old railroad apartments, one room leading into the next. As I neared the third room, I heard two voices. The woman was obviously agitated, and the man was trying to calm her down. I moved a little closer and then stopped to listen. It was Lee and that heavy girl. I didn't know her name, but she was upset about something. I leaned toward the cracked door, straining to hear more.

"Babe, there's nothing to worry about. We're just friends. That's all. She's just out here for the day."

The girl said something in a sarcastic tone, but I couldn't make it out. I pressed in closer. Without warning the rough wood hit me in the face as she flung open the door and bolted through. I stumbled backward, tripping over my feet and hitting the wall behind me. Her eyes shot right through me. She was big, and she was mad.

"You better watch your step," she said. I clutched the wall behind me and tried to straighten up. Her eyes told me she wasn't talking about me falling in the hall.

Lee heard the thud and came out the door. "Hey, you okay?" He tried to help me up and then turned to face the girl. "Angela, I will talk to you later. It's time to go."

"I'll go when I want to go." She turned to face me. "Hey, city girl, you better get going yourself. Don't want to miss your train."

She headed out through the last two rooms and out the back door with a slam.

Lee and I walked back to the front of the house to find George in the kitchen. I was afraid to ask but wanted to know. "Lee, what was that all about?"

"Oh, nothing, Just Angela being Angela. She gets crazy sometimes. But it's cool."

It didn't feel cool. She seemed to have a connection to Lee, but she didn't fit his type.

"How do you know her?"

"She's a friend. She lives down the beach and works at the laundromat. She's really sweet once you get to know her. Funny too. She gets lonely sometimes working at the mat all day. I go in to do my laundry, and we talk. It's no big deal."

It looked like a big deal to Angela. I wanted to ask more questions but decided not to probe. Lee already seemed a little irritated.

"Come on. Let's get out of here," said Lee.

He grabbed my hand and led me to the garage.

CHAPTER 6

Friday finally arrived, and I wanted to be home. The train was still at Track 17. *Thank God I didn't miss it.* I crossed the platform and entered the first open compartment. The car was packed. Even though I was almost four months pregnant and none of my clothes fit, I still wasn't eliciting any gentleman to give me his seat. The chilly November air forced me to wear my long wool coat, making my pregnancy undetectable.

I liked being invisible. Not many people knew yet, not even my parents. I had to tell them, but fear kept me from dialing their number.

I walked down the aisle to the door leading to the next car. I reached to push it open just as the train's engine clanked into gear. The sudden motion threw me off balance, and I fell forward, dropping my books. My abrupt entrance into the next car was met with grumpy stares. One man was sitting in the first row, buttoned to his chin in black wool, with a black leather bag resting on his lap. His thick raven hair hung over his tortoise-shell frames.

He glanced at me. His eyes first gazed at my face and then followed the buttons of my coat, stopping at my belly. He paused, staring for a moment at the large plastic button, as if he saw something. He quickly diverted his eyes, cleared his throat, and bent down to pick up my books.

I watched him read the titles as he picked up each paperback. Desperate to keep my secret hidden, I knelt down, trying to grab them from his polite hands. But his long arm had already retrieved them, and he surrendered them into my arms with a smile that softened his stern face.

I tucked *What to Expect When You Are Expecting* and *Modern Baby Names* into my coat. I glared at him, wondering if he noticed my bare left ring finger. My face flushed with shame.

"Miss, let me help you up," he said.

Oh, great, I thought. *He called me Miss. He knows.*

He assisted me to my feet and offered me the empty window seat next to his. I nodded, turned sideways, plopping into the seat, spilling myself all over my seat and his. My red scarf landed in his lap.

"Sorry, excuse me," I said.

He politely laid my scarf on my shoulder. "It's okay. These seats are small."

I glued my eyes to the seatback in front of me, praying he would not start a conversation. But my petition was ignored.

"My name is Charlie, what's yours?"

"Grace."

"Pleasure to meet you Grace. "I see your book. Mind if I ask how far along are you?"

I wanted to escape—or disappear. I stared out the window as the train rocked along the tracks, pretending I didn't hear him. But he patiently waited for my answer. I could feel the energy of his eyes on my face.

"About sixteen weeks," I said without looking at him.

He did a quick calculation in his head. "So you're into your fourth month. That's great! Almost halfway there." Like it was a trip to Disney World.

I slowly turned my head to look at him. *Why on earth was he so happy about it?* "Yeah, halfway there," I echoed his words.

He looked at me as if he was studying me. I felt naked, like he could read my thoughts. He didn't blink. He just stared, searching my cold face.

I squirmed in my seat and opened my book of baby names.

"Have you chosen one yet?" he asked.

"Chosen one?" I asked back.

"A name. Have you chosen a name for your baby? The name is important. Be sure to understand its meaning," he said with authority.

"Okay," I said, looking at him. I hadn't decided on one yet. I flipped through the book, pretending to read. He glanced over my shoulder.

"Boy names or girl?" he asked with the smile of a five-year-old.

"I'm not sure yet. Don't know till I see it—that is, if I see it," I mumbled, making sure to say the last part under my breath. He looked confused. His mouth opened to ask another question I was not prepared to answer. I slammed the book shut, sat up a little straighter, and planned my diversion. "So you have kids?" I asked.

He erupted into laughter. "Oh, no! Heavens, no. No, I don't have kids." I glanced at his left hand. Naked as mine. For someone so excited about my kid, I was baffled that he didn't have his own. He added, "No, no, the diocese frowns on priests fathering children."

I sat up even straighter. Holy cow. I was sitting next to a priest. What were the odds? The condemnation pushed me back down in my seat. He sensed my fear.

He leaned over, gently placing his hand on top of mine for a second, and said, "Relax. All is well."

Maybe in his world all was well, but not in mine. Mine was all is hell. I was sure I was on my way there, skipping right past purgatory.

"You're doing a brave thing, choosing to have this baby," he whispered. I didn't feel brave. I was scared every day. "Do you have family here?" he asked.

"No, they are in Colorado."

"Colorado? Is that where you are from? You are far away from home."

"Yeah, I've been in New York for three years. Left right after college."

"What brought you to the city?"

"Love," I said as if I didn't believe it. "My boyfriend from college is from here. I came out to be with him," I said.

"Ahh," he said as if he put the puzzle together.

"But we broke up last summer." I looked at his face. That puzzle piece was not going to fit in his world.

"Oh," was all he said. His disappointment hung in the air like thick smog. I tried to save face.

"I loved him. I did. He was my first love. We were going to get married. He even gave me a ring."

"So what happened?" he asked.

"He was a couple of years older than me. He'd been in the city two years working before I came."

"What did he do?" he asked.

"Real estate, commercial," I said with a grain of pride. "But when I came out to be with him, it was different. He was different."

"People change."

"Yeah, they do," I said, eyes downcast.

He looked up toward the ceiling of the train and didn't ask me the details. I waited, but nothing. I realized he was waiting on me. At first I hesitated. But something nudged me to continue. It felt safe. I poured out my life story. He listened patiently without judgment. I almost forgot he was a priest. When I was finished I let out a heavy sigh. It was the same feeling I got when I was young and I had to go to confession. I started out scared, but then I felt better—lighter.

He gave me a card with his number on it. "Call me anytime," he said. "My parish is only a few blocks away from the last stop on the 4 train in the Bronx."

We sat in silence for a few moments.

"Please," he implored. "Come visit."

I nodded yes, blinking away my tears. I hadn't been in church in a couple of years. All the years of Catholic school had worn me out. I was so tired of trying to be good and perfect. I always felt like I was failing, so I stopped going to church. It was too late to catch up. My transgressions outweighed my goodness. And now, with "unwed mother" added to my long list of sins, I thought it was too late. I was a lost cause.

Father Charlie gave me his handkerchief. It was white and clean. I wiped my eyes and dabbed my nose then carefully folded it into a square and handed it back to him. For a second I thought of my dad. He always had white handkerchiefs in his pocket. When I was little and cried, he would take it out and let me blow my nose. He didn't care that all my snot had soiled it. He would wad it back up and stick it back in his pocket.

The train was approaching Father Charlie's stop. He stood up and looked me in the eyes. "Please come see me. Anytime."

"Okay," I said, forcing a half smile. He stepped off the train and disappeared into the herd of other commuters. I stuck his card in my book of baby names. Exhaling deeply, I closed my eyes. Four more stops before mine. I slept.

CHAPTER 7

"Botanical Gardens!"

The conductor's voice startled me out of sleep. I felt as if I had slept for eight hours, but it had only been twenty minutes. I tried to peel open my eyes. My cheek was damp from drool. Again, the conductor's voice crackled on the loud speaker, "Station 679!"

I missed my stop. There was nothing I could do. I had to ride to the end of the line and then catch the train on the opposite side of the tracks. It was only one more stop, but that was Fordham. Not the best place to be getting off at 9:30 at night. I looked around the car. It was empty except for a middle-aged man sitting three rows up. I buttoned the top button on my wool coat and wrapped my scarf securely around my neck. I shoved the two books into my shoulder bag and held it close to my body.

For the first time in a long time, I prayed.

Dear God, if You are listening and aren't too angry with me, will You help me? Please, please protect me. Keep me safe. I'm scared to get off at Fordham. I'm so sorry. I know I'm a screw-up, but please do it for the baby.

I discreetly crossed myself and ended my prayer with an audible "Amen."

The train screeched to a stop. "Last stop, Fordham!"

I glanced at the man. I waited for him to get up first, and then followed him out the door onto the platform. He had a short, quick gait. I tried to keep up with him, practically running down the stairs. The tracks were empty, and so were the staircases. At the bottom he made a quick right and hiked out to a parking lot. There were only about five cars sitting in the darkness. How I wished I had a car. I stopped and looked to my left. There was no staircase up to the opposite track. How would I catch the train going back toward the Bronx? Panic kicked me into high gear. I felt my heart pounding under all the thick layers. This was not a part of the Bronx that welcomed a pretty fair-skinned girl.

Breathe, just breathe. I blinked my eyes, trying to refocus. To my left I saw a wall painted with orange graffiti. I felt drawn to the bright color in the darkness. I had no idea where I was or where I was going. I followed the pull toward the angry orange letters. I looked to my left, then right, and left again, as my mom taught me to do when crossing the street as a young child. But there was no street. Only empty pavement and darkness.

One last look behind me, and then I went for it. I scuffled, clutching my bag to my chest, and made it to the side of the orange wall. I was breathing heavily, as if I had just run the fifty-yard dash. I paused and tried to focus on the graffiti letters, but they were cryptic to me. My eyes traveled down the side of the building, trying to make sense of the scrawl. The paint ended. There appeared to be a break in the wall. I walked closer and saw the opening to a tunnel. I ran toward the entrance and stopped short. I peered through the cement cave but could not see a thing. In the far distance was a patch of light, marking the other end. It was the in-between I was worried about.

My heartbeat escalated again. I knew the tracks had to be on the other side of that tunnel, but fear froze me in place. I looked back. Maybe I could run back to the parking lot and bum a ride with the owner of one of the empty cars. I felt that strange magnetic pull again. The force was stronger now, almost pushing me forward. I closed my eyes tightly, secured my bag over one shoulder and my neck. I patted my belly and looked up toward the vacant sky. *Please, God, get me through to the other side.*

I walked, taking huge steps, counting each one out loud to distract myself from the fear. "One, two, three, four, five, six, seven, eight. One, two, three, four, five, six, seven, eight." I repeated my steps in sets of eight, staring down at my feet. After about ten sets I stopped to calculate my distance. It was hard to calculate in the dark. Maybe I should take bigger steps. Contemplating the math, I was lost in my head.

Once again I felt a presence. It was strong enough to stop my methodical counting. It felt like a breeze at first. But breezes are nice, and this force did not feel pleasant. I turned quickly, trying to catch a shadow behind me, but saw nothing. I lost my count. Everything stopped. The breeze got stronger. I stood still, not daring to move a muscle. My mind took me back to when I was ten and played statue in the yard with my sisters and the neighbor kids. I would run until I felt a touch and then had to freeze in that exact position.

Here I was, frozen in place. I even felt the baby freeze inside me.

And then they came.

Like a flock of blackbirds. Yelling and chanting in unison. One voice was higher and louder than the others, speaking in a foreign tongue. It sounded more pleading than speaking. I squeezed my eyelids together, one arm protecting my tummy.

The voices were closer, and I felt the pounding of boots on the pavement.

"Pacifico! Pacifico! Pacifico!" the boy with the accent boomed in my ear, and then he passed. I felt a rush of air, and peeled open one eye to peek.

All I could see was a glimpse of dark skin and a boy about twenty wearing a sweatshirt running toward the opening of the tunnel. I started to lift my leg to take a step. The boy had vanished, so I lifted my other leg and took a long step toward the dim light. The breeze came back.

The flock entered the cave. I stared in the darkness trying to see. It was a blur of dark bodies coming toward me, loud and fast like a subway train. I clutched my bag and lunged forward. My face hit the damp brick wall.

I held my breath, what I thought would be my last breath, and clutched my belly while the flock of boys sprinted by me.

The chanting faded into the distance, but I was too afraid to open my eyes and turn around. My nose pressed into the wall, I felt cold tears drop, plopping to the pavement. I started to count. This time I did not stop until I reached one hundred. Thoughts raced through my mind. *Was I alone? Where did they go?* I felt like running, but all the life force had drained out of my legs. They felt heavy like bricks.

Finally I began again with slow, steady steps. "One, two, three, four, five, six, seven, eight," I counted out loud, and the sound of my voice calmed my body.

My eyes stayed focused on my feet. I did not know I reached the end of the tunnel until the color of concrete changed from a dark ash to a pale, dirty brown. I looked up and saw the metal railing to the cement stairs leading to the other side of the tracks. I grabbed the railing like it was a life preserver and pulled my heavy body up the stairs.

I took four steps and then collapsed on the closest bench. I had no idea when the next train was coming or even if one was coming. I hugged my belly and wiped my tear-stained face with my sleeve. I could only sit and wait.

I stared down the metal rails, willing a train to come. *Come on, come on, come on*, I chanted to myself.

A whistle broke through the silence, followed by two more. I stood up and walked to the other end of the platform looking for a train. I saw nothing. I leaned over the metal railing of the exit staircase and heard voices echoing down the corridor. This time they were voices I could understand.

Not wanting to miss the train, I scuttled back to my bench. The voices got louder. *Come on, come on*, I chanted once more, beckoning the train.

Boots scraped the concrete, and I heard pounding as a man ran up the stairs. It was one of the boys.

But his gait slowed down as he approached the platform. This time he saw me and looked right into my eyes. I tried to look away but couldn't. Fresh blood dripped down his face. His black hoodie was covered with a dark red coating. He stumbled toward me.

Quickly I bounced off the bench and leaned into the railing. The bloody boy lunged toward my bench but fell to his knees.

Four more deep voices interrupted, and men bounded up the stairs. Two were in blue uniforms, and they were escorting two more in black hooded sweatshirts. Their hands were cuffed behind their backs, and they struggled in their walk, resisting the movement forward.

One of the men in the blue uniforms came near me. I let myself exhale in relief. His eyes met mine, and I used them to beckon help. He looked at me, but not in a helpful "Are you okay?" way. His hungry eyes grazed my body, and he slowly grinned. He took a step toward me, and I reached for the bench with the bloody boy. He sat there giving me the same plea for help I gave the man in blue. Close up I could see that one eye was swollen shut. Blood from the crown of his head dripped down his face and dried on his cheeks. His jeans were torn and boots ripped off his bare, bloody feet. He looked broken.

Annoyed with me, the officer yelled, "You gonna sit with the bloody loser over there?"

I could smell whiskey on his breath, and the stench almost made me puke. I scooted closer to the boy, being careful not to touch his body.

"Get close, sweetness," sneered the cop. "You're in the wrong neighborhood, my darling."

I pretended to ignore him, hoping he would follow the others and go away. In the distance I heard a car door slam. I looked back toward the stairs and then at the drunken cop glaring at my belly.

"Glen, get your sorry butt down these stairs!" another man yelled from below. Glen looked up and then back at me. "It's your lucky day, sister."

The boy looked at Glen and said something I could not understand and spit on the ground. Glen lifted his arm to take a swing at the boy but lost his balance as the other officer bounded up the stairs in time to see him face plant into the pavement.

The officer looked at me and then the boy and back to me. "You all right, young lady?" I was too bewildered and exhausted to speak. I nodded my head.

"The 11:17 should be here any minute. Get on that train, and you'll be fine."

He picked up the groaning Glen from the pavement and dragged him down the stairs half conscious.

The silence was loud. I sat down on the opposite end of the bench. I looked at the boy cautiously, hoping he was still conscious. He lifted his drooping head about an inch, and with the one eye that was not swollen shut he met mine. He muttered words under his breath in a heavy accent I could barely understand. I strained to listen.

All I could make out were a few words: "Why do they do the hurt?" He shook his head back and forth entranced in his chant.

I looked down the tracks hoping the train would soon appear. Not so much for me—this boy needed a hospital. His head dropped low again, and he appeared to sleep.

I leaned back and shut my eyes, trying to make sense of the night's events. How one missed train stop could turn life down a dark road. Heaviness covered my body, and I let my mind drift and my body go. Then the train came screaming down the tracks, startling us both straight up and wide-eyed. It screeched to a halt, and we both climbed aboard.

Bryan made his rounds through the train cars, punching tickets and checking seats. At first he walked past me and then paused, backed up, and did a double take. "Deary, what in God's holy name are you doing here at this ungodly hour?"

I told him how I'd fallen asleep on the Metro and missed my stop. And my walk through the tunnel, the gang of guys, and the drunken officer.

He listened and sipped his coffee. "Here, take a sip," he said, offering me his cup. "You need this more than me." The coffee calmed my shaking body.

"You're lucky you made it back on this train in one piece," he scolded.

I looked up at him. "I know."

"Fordham is crawling with gangbangers. You need to stay awake, darling. Did they take anything? Your purse?" He looked me over, checking me out.

"No. I'm fine. There was a gang of them. Boys in black. But they just ran through me. It was like they didn't even see me. Like I was surrounded by some kind of force field."

"Force field?" he asked. "You getting all Trekky on me?"

"No, no, it was not like that. It was more like a covering. I felt hidden. I can't explain it."

Bryan winked at me. "Maybe it was your guardian angel."

My eyes widened. I had not thought of that. "Maybe it was." For the first time I contemplated the existence of angels.

"Well, whatever it was, you were spared. I'm glad you are okay. I gotta make the rounds but will be back to make sure you get off at the right stop," he said.

I sat back and sipped the coffee he left for me to finish. I thought about the kid covered in blood. He was on this train somewhere. I wondered if he had a guardian angel. I looked down at my belly. "You okay in there, baby?" I whispered.

CHAPTER 8

The early Saturday sun danced in my window. I peeked at the brightness, and for a second, I thought I was someplace else. Maybe the past few weeks had been a bad dream. The sun sent a beam of light through my window glass, creating a bright path on my hardwood floors. I turned over to bask in the warmth of the ray. I imagined I was back on the beach with Lee. My face relaxed into a soft smile. Two seconds later I felt a quiver in my belly.

Reality was kicking me in the gut. As fast as the ray of sun entered my room, it disappeared behind a bully cloud. Something jabbed my insides again. I laid still, secretly hoping it was detaching from the walls of my uterus and would slip away. I could not accept that a baby was inside me. I wanted to be free of my fate and fear.

But then I remembered I was in my fifth month. Could this quiver be a kick? I gently rubbed my bare belly, coaxing it to move again. Nothing. I waited. Afraid to move, I lay still. My belly felt round and tight. The skin stretched smooth. It felt hard. With one hand supporting my body I rolled onto my side and pushed myself up to sitting. The quiver came again, sending a shooting pain down my legs. Did I dare move again? But I had to pee. The pressure was pounding. Slowly I stood, cradling my baby bump with both hands. I walked to the bathroom.

A knock at the door interrupted my privacy. I slid my sock-covered feet on the wood floors toward the front door. Pressing my right eye through the peephole, I called, "Who is it?"

I heard Sheila call out in her sweet Irish accent, "It's your lovely neighbor. Checkin' in on you, deary."

Bryan and Sheila had moved into my building about six months before. They were right off the boat from Ireland. Sheila came downstairs one Saturday night and knocked repeatedly on my door. She was frantic as she stood outside with a head full of pink rollers. I opened the door with curiosity.

"Yes?" I asked.

In one long breath with an Irish accent, she said, "Hi, I'm yer neighbor two flurs up. 5B. I've seen ya girls around, and ya look so pleasant. I was wonderin'—I'm in a bit of a pickle; I need a sitter to look after me wee ones. I have four, tree boys and a wee baby girl. Me sitter, she didn't show, and I'm meeting the girls down at Patty's. Sherrie's husband's playin' tonight, and, well, I need a little help. They'll be no trouble at all, would ya do it? Please?"

Her big baby blues pleaded with me to say yes. How could I say no?

"Okay, I guess I could do it," I said.

I was amazed that she would ask a complete stranger to watch her kids, but if she trusted me, then I better do it.

"What time do you need me?" I asked.

"Umm, now would be lovely," she answered.

"Okay. Let me grab my keys." I slipped on my shoes, shut the door behind me, and followed her up the stairs. She talked non-stop about her kids the whole way to the fifth floor. I followed her into her apartment, and she led me back to the bathroom to give me the instructions as she painted blue shadow on her lids and squeezed her soft tummy into a pair of tight-fitting jeans. The zipper pushed up the roll of fat until it was hanging over the top seam.

She looked down and laughed. "That's what four babies will do to ya."

I grimaced in horror. I couldn't take my eyes off her roll top. She smiled and pulled a long navy knit sweater over her head. The top skimmed her hips and hid the tummy roll. Next, she pulled out her pink rollers, throwing the clips into the bathroom sink, ran a brush through her chestnut hair, and then twisted it up into a high ponytail. Last she puckered her lips and applied an apricot lipstick that gave her an instant plumpy lip look. She stepped back, taking one final look in the mirror. She smiled with approval with one last adjustment of her sweater.

"Not bad, me dear." Her silver blue eyes glistened in the light.

Off she went down the hall in her black high-heeled boots. I struggled to keep up as she turned the corner and led me into another small room.

"Hi, boys!" She smiled.

"Mama!" they yelled in unison.

The littlest one with curly blond hair said, "You look pretty, Mama."

"That one is Sean, he's tree," said Sheila. "Say hello to Miss Gracie. She's goin' to watch ya tonight." Sean stared at me with a little fear in his green eyes. He wasn't sure about this arrangement.

"That's Scott, he's four, and Michael is in the toy box. He will be two in November." She whipped around and led me to another room. "The baby is in here, me and Bryan's room." She entered on tiptoe peeking into the small crib. In a whisper she said, "This is baby Amy. Her bottle is in the fridge. Give it to her at eight."

She air-kissed the sleeping baby's head. "Well, that should do it. There's a Coke for ya in the kitchen, and the boys go down at 8:30. I'll be down at Patty's if ya need anythin'." Sheila grabbed a black leather bomber jacket from the hall closet and yelled in her sweet accent, "'Bye, boys! Be good for Gracie." She smiled with her eyes. "Any questions?"

She blew kisses in the air and was out the door before I could think of what to ask. What did I get myself into? I stood in the living room, not knowing where to begin. The boys or the baby? Just then the baby let out a cry. My decision was made for me.

It had been six months since that night and we had become good friends.

Sheila knocked harder. I unhinged the metal floor bar, turned the three dead bolts and opened the door to Sheila's child-like grin.

"Ya want to come up for a spot of tea and wee chat?" she said. "Bryan told me about what happened on the train. Ya poor girl. Come on now, grab your slippers and come on up for a bit."

I dragged myself up the two flights to her apartment. Once inside, she led me into the kitchen. She pulled out a blue wooden chair. "Sit. Here ya are."

I squeezed my big belly between the round table and chair and tried to get comfortable. The table was a deep cherry red, covered with nicks and stains, pushed up against the kitchen wall right under a window. The black kettle was on the stove, and Sheila plunked down two ivory cups painted with faded roses. She set a bowl of sugar and small pitcher of cream in front of the cups.

"Tea will be done in a sec," she said as she reached over the table to lift up the window. A burst of wind sent a chill into the room. Even though the day had been sunny and unseasonably warm for February, the night air was cold. She grabbed a chipped silver handle and turned it clockwise several times. A frayed rope moved toward us with bright cotton towels hanging in frozen stillness. "I meant to take these in earlier, but me boys kept me runnin' all day."

As the towels entered through the window single file she yanked them off the line and then sent it back out into the dark sky. She folded a crisp tea towel and laid it on the center of the table. The whistle started to blow, and she grabbed the kettle off the stove with a mitted hand. With the care of a nurse, she poured the steaming water into our cups, not spilling a drop. She smoothed out the linen towel and set two tiny silver spoons on top.

Pleased with her work, she sat in the opposite chair and took a sip of her steaming tea. Her eyes met mine, and she asked the question. "So tell me about this fella. Who is he? And what exactly is the problem?" Her eyes lit up her cheeks. Her skin, so white and smooth, made her look much younger than thirty-eight.

"Soo. . . ," she continued. "This fella, Lee is his name? Where is he? He going to help ya?"

I dropped some sugar into my cup and watched it melt in the steam. "I don't know. He won't return my calls."

"Won't return ye calls, huh? Does he know about the wee one?" she asked.

"Yes, I told him."

Sheila stared at her tea and shook her head. "The coward!" she exclaimed. "Don't he know he's a da now? He must step up and be a man."

I took a sip of my tea, but it was still too hot to drink so I set it down. "Yeah, well, I don't think Lee wants to be a daddy," I said.

"He wanted me to take care of it, you know, but he didn't even offer money to pay for the procedure."

"I know, sweetie, but you didn't do it. You did the right thing. You are me brave child. God be pleased."

I stared at her. It was hard for me to believe God could be pleased with me. Sheila read my thoughts.

"He is, ya know. He's blessing ya with this wee baby."

I stared out the window. She knew I didn't believe it.

"Wait one minute," she said. "I will be right back."

Sheila disappeared into the front room. A few minutes later she came back with her arms piled high with baby gear. She laid the bundle at my feet.

"I saved a few things for ya, my dear." She picked up each item one at a time, describing it in detail, including which one of her babies had used it and a story to go along with it. She lifted up a long, plastic tub. "Here's a wee baby bath for ya. All my little ones washed in this tub. Ohh, how little Amy loved her bath," she said. "And here are some bottles, boiled them clean yesterday, good as new." She reached down for some nappys to hand me. "I know they're cloth, but with four young'uns we couldn't afford the Pampers. They also make good spit-up rags."

"Spit-up rags?" I asked. "Oh, I can't wait to use those." I squinted my eyes.

"Oh, you just wait and see," she said with a knowing smile. "You're gonna make a fine mama."

I sipped my tea in silence, doubting I was fine in any way.

Sheila got busy folding the diapers into neat little squares. Then she looked up suddenly. "Do ya have a coach?"

"Coach? What do you mean? Why do I need a coach?"

"You know, a birthing coach. Someone to help you with ya breathing."

I looked at her like she was crazy. "My breathing?" I asked. "So I am going to need help breathing?"

Sheila laughed at my naivete. "Only through the contractions, my dear. You will need someone to help ya focus. Hold your hand. Normally that's the daddy's job." Her laughter stopped.

I could not believe this was happening. I felt smothered with all the baby items at my feet. "Move this stuff, Sheila," I said. "I'm covered over here."

She ignored my lack of gratitude. "Oh, child, don't ya worry. I've had four wee ones. I'll be there to help you. You're not alone."

She placed her hand on top of mine, and the warmth of her touch melted my anger into tears. I shook my head. "All I seem to do is cry these days. I cry at anything."

"That's just the hormones, my love. It's all part of the package," she said. "And look at the night ya just survived. Bryan told me all about it. It's by God's grace ya are still alive to sit here in my kitchen and those hoodlums didn't touch ya."

"I know," I said. "It was crazy. I'm still in shock. I keep thinking of the boy and all that blood. I hope he's okay."

"Well, the main thing is that ya and that wee one are okay. Ya need to be extra careful now, love. Extra careful."

"Yeah, extra careful," I repeated. "I wish someone would have told me that about five months ago. Then I wouldn't be in this mess.

"Oh, child, a baby is not a mess. It's a gift from God."

It was hard for me to believe God had anything to do with this. "Well," I said, "if this is a gift, can I return it?"

Sheila's eyes got big. "No, my dear, don't speak such a thing! You will see. In time, my love. In time."

We stirred more sugar and sipped more tea. Time seemed to stop. I sat suspended in Sheila's kitchen, like the tea towels hanging in midair between buildings. All I could do was sit and wait. I desperately dreamed of someone big and strong, reaching out the window and reeling me in to safety.

CHAPTER 9

On Sunday morning the streets were quiet. Everyone was recovering from their Saturday night binge. I decided to venture out because we had no food in the house. Michelle had been traveling a lot with her job and spending the weekends with her sister in PA. We were out of bread, milk and coffee. I laced up my shoes and headed down stairs. The brisk air slapped me in the face as I entered the courtyard. I buttoned my top button wishing I'd remembered my scarf. But it wasn't worth climbing three flights of stairs to fetch. I was only going to the corner deli anyway.

The wind picked up speed, lifting trash up out of the gutters. Beer bottles rolled and rattled against the curb. Not a soul looked awake except me. I shoved my hands into my wool pockets as I treaded along to the deli. I could do this walk in my sleep and had done it many times, barely awake, after late Saturday nights.

Four more steps, turn the corner, and I was in. I couldn't wait to feel the heat inside.

I leaned into the door with all my weight, but it resisted my push. I tried again, but the door didn't budge. Confused, I pressed my face into the glass. It was dark and dead. Stepping back, I glanced in the window at a hand-written sign. In black sharpie letters it said, *Closed today for Uncle Jack's funeral. Will re-open 6 am Monday.*

I groaned in frustration and re-read the sign. I wondered, *Do I know Uncle Jack?*

I knew Paulee, the owner, and his wife, Nina. I stood on the sidewalk, indecisive. *Should I walk home or trek another seven blocks to Mackenzie's?* I counted my cash. Barely twenty dollars. At least I could get something hot to drink. I headed toward the street and passed the subway stop into the city, but it looked abandoned. The wind picked up again. Now I wished I had gone back for my scarf. I kept walking, staring at the sidewalk squares, trying to ignore the fact that I was freezing. As I inhaled, the cold air cut my throat. I couldn't breathe. I couldn't walk five more long blocks. My heart was pounding, and I was out of breath. "You weigh a ton," I said to the baby in my belly.

Five seconds later sheets of sleet hung in the sky, and sharp pieces of ice hit my cheeks. "That's it," I said to the baby. "We are finding cover."

I ducked under the first awning I saw and turned away from the wind so I could catch my breath. The storefront was closed, but the awning provided a partial shelter from the storm.

I wish I was in the city. Then I would just hail a cab.

Seconds later a car whizzed by me. I looked up. It was long and black—a hearse. I wondered if Uncle Jack was inside. Then I remembered the church. Father Charlie's church. He said it was only a few blocks from the subway stop in my neighborhood.

I decided to step out from my cover and make a run for the corner. *Which way?* I wondered. *Which way is the church?* In response to my silent question, a gust of wind sent a beer bottle rolling my way. It stopped right in front of my feet. Its neck pointed left, to the east.

What the heck, I thought. *I have nothing to lose.*

I walked east.

This part of the neighborhood was new to me. I usually went no further than the subway stop. The buildings looked unfamiliar. I felt a new strength in my stride. A few more cars were on this street. A cab sped by. I kept walking until I was forced to stop at the light. *Do I turn?* I asked. Before I could answer myself, my legs started walking again, straight ahead, like they knew something I didn't. My pace quickened as I crossed another block. Two buildings down on the left, a group of people huddled together. I crossed over to the south side of the street, and as I neared the huddle, bells began ringing. The chimes declared the time. Ten o'clock. Rising high in the sky was a steeple. *This has to be it.* I felt myself racing to the stone steps. I slowed down as I trudged up the stairs, cradling my baby belly in my arms. At the top I stopped at two large wooden doors. The walls of the church were red brick, and cemented high above the door was a gold-plated sign: *Welcome to Saint Michael's.*

Without thinking, I bolted in through one door, eager to finally find warmth. My embarrassment stopped me as I realized I had entered mid-mass. Everyone was sitting properly in pews, listening to the sermon. Only a few heads turned back to look at the intruder. A kind, elderly gentleman silently walked toward me and in a whisper said, "This is why we shut this door. It's a bit brisk out today, miss." He gently touched my arm, encouraging me to release my grip on the door handle. He took my arm and led me toward a door on the far right. He opened it, pointed to an open space in the second to last pew, and nodded his head to encourage me to sit.

I wanted to bolt back out the door. But my numb fingers and toes trumped my humiliation. I succumbed to the hard, but warm, pew.

"Excuse me," I muttered as I passed the old woman in gray wool sitting on the end. I slunk down in the pew, trying to be inconspicuous. A few more heads turned to watch me but turned back toward the altar, as if led by a conductor.

I was so far back that it was hard to see. But the priest looked young and familiar. It was not until I listened to his voice that I realized it was Father Charlie from the train. He was in the middle of a story. It was about a father whose son came home after squandering all of his money.

It had been a few years since I sat in a church. But it was like riding a bike—all the moves quickly came back to me. Even the prayers I had memorized in Catholic school seemed to jump to the front of my brain. And soon the Apostle's Creed was flowing from my chapped lips.

Stand, sit, kneel, and then stand again. It was time for the "Our Father." People stood, linked together by a chain of clasped hands.

I glanced at the old woman in gray, wanting to extend my hand toward her. But she made it clear with her hands clasped in front, that she wanted nothing to do with my cold hand.

I bowed my head and linked my fingers together, resting them under my belly. From memory the words floated out of my mouth. "Our Father, who art in heaven. Hallowed be thy name. Thy kingdom come, thy will be done, on earth as it is in heaven."

I paused, opened my eyes, and stared at the cross. I wondered, *Was it possible to know God's will? And if so, could a sinful human actually do God's will?*

It was all too overwhelming to ponder.

The mass ended. "Go in peace."

These final words brought back my wandering mind. Without thinking I uttered, "Thanks be to God." As the choir delivered the closing hymn, I closed my eyes. I waited until all the worshippers had vanished through the front hall. Finally I opened my eyes. The church looked different without all the people. The only light seeped through the stained glass. I breathed in the stillness. *This must be what peace feels like.* I gazed up and down the pews to see if I was alone. It was barren except for a straggler way up in the front pew.

I saw the shadow of an old woman sitting hunched over in her pew. All I could see was the blue wool of her coat. Her head was bowed, hidden behind the blue hunch in her back. She looked like one of the statues up on the altar. Stiff and surreal.

I slid back into the pew. For a few moments I felt safe. It was an unfamiliar feeling. Confusion, fear, and loneliness seemed to be my faithful friends. Safety, security, and peace—these were strangers I had not seen in a long while. I liked their feel, their presence. I wished I could wrap them up and take them home. But once I left this holy place they would flee. So I sat and soaked, absorbing all I could before the bells would tell me it was time to leave.

The lady in blue peeled up out of her pew first. She struggled in her walk, grabbing the corner of each pew as she limped down the aisle. Her eyes were focused on the floor.

I watched her move, feeling with each unsteady step the pain she must have felt. Halfway down the aisle, she stopped. She stood still as the statue of the Virgin Mary.

I stared, certain she was oblivious to my presence.

In one slight movement her body unwound, and she stood straight as a soldier, gazing at me with eyes that matched her coat.

I'd been caught. All my secrets were revealed in this mysterious moment of knowing. She kept looking at me. Her lips pressed together. Her eyes never blinked.

Finding my bravery, I met her gaze. She looked into my soul, and I looked into hers. She did not look real. She let out a loud cry, more like a moan. She fell to her knees with her hands stretching up toward the domed ceiling. Her frail body shook as she moaned. One of her hands beckoned me to come closer.

With my courage now broken, I hesitated. But she moaned louder. Her plea brought me to my feet, and I walked toward her. I stopped short of her and kneeled on one knee, holding onto the pew. Her moaning grew louder, and I was afraid for her life. I reached out my hand. In a whisper I asked, "What can I do? I can help you. Tell me what you need."

Her moaning quieted to a whisper. She reached out her wrinkled hand and grabbed mine. She held on to it with a life-saving grip. "No, my child. I am the one that offers the help. I intercede for you, young one."

In her next breath words poured from her mouth with a powerful force. She spoke a language I had never heard. It sounded like French mixed with Latin and a little Indian chant thrown in for punctuation.

"Kin da la, sheekitah, ooh fa so kins da come la sheekitah."

She repeated the same words and syllables over and over. Each time they became louder and more powerful. At first fear tried to attack me. But then the presence of peace blew it away. I listened, closing my eyes out of respect, as I let her pray her language of love over me.

The vibration of the chant descended, and the grip on my hand released. Her song was now a whisper, and tears rolled down her cheeks. Her head lifted, and she raised her bony arm to touch my face. Her fragile fingers stroked my cheek, and her voice softened. "You are the one who needs a rescuer, my child. And He has come."

Startled, I pulled my hand away. Her creaking body leaned forward, reaching toward me. "Don't be afraid, my child—come, come near me."

"I'm not afraid," I lied. "I'm okay. You don't have to—"

She interrupted me with a laugh that broke the stillness. "A blind woman could see what I see, child. I may be old, but I still have eyes to see and ears to hear," she said. Her gaze traveled to my belly. She smiled. "Yes, I still have eyes that see, my child."

Just then the church bells vibrated through the vacant cathedral. The doors would be locked soon. *We must leave now,* was all I could think.

Her gaze grew stronger. I looked at her again. I felt as if I had known her in some other lifetime. I could feel her compassion, her heartbeat.

"Now you do not see," she started again. "But soon your eyes will be opened, and you will see clearly."

See what? I thought.

The old woman interrupted my thoughts and grabbed my hand again. She spoke with authority: "Now you see but a poor reflection as in a mirror; then you shall see face-to-face."

She paused and looked up into my eyes. "Now, my dear child, you only know in part; but then you shall know fully, even as you are fully known."

I didn't remember this class in Catholic school. She had lost me. But even though I did not know what her words meant, I felt the sweetness of them. I believed they were truth—I felt the pure presence of love.

Our unscheduled prayer session was interrupted by strong footsteps approaching the front of the church. I turned to look and saw a tall man coming toward us.

"It's time," she said. She reached up and kissed my cheek. Then she shimmied through the pew with a newfound youthfulness and exited through the side door. I stood in the aisle, turning toward the man approaching.

"We have to lock up the church, my dear," he said. The lights were dim, and I could tell he did not recognize me from the train ride.

"Father Charlie, it's me, from the train," I said, hoping he would remember.

"Oh, yes! Yes, it is you, my dear Gracie," he said.

A smile softened my face. I was surprised by how good it felt to see him. He led me out of the church and around the back to a little stone cottage. I waited as he fumbled for his keys in his pocket. In silence he unlocked the door and led me into his home. In the entry way there was one lone table with a vase half-filled with water. I followed him to the next room. A living area with two green-velvet, high-back chairs, a table and a desk. All the wood was dark. Father Charlie motioned for me to sit in the chair. And then he vanished down a long hallway.

I let out a heavy sigh and sank deep into the crushed velvet. Father Charlie came back into the study with two cups of tea. He put one porcelain cup in front of me, and he held his as he sat down and crossed his legs.

"I am so happy you came to visit my church," he said. "Did you enjoy the service? If I had known you were coming, I would have met you earlier."

If I had known I was coming, then maybe I would have called him, I thought. "Well, it was kind of a last-minute decision," I said.

"Well, it is good to see you, my dear. How is that child doing?"

"Child?" I was confused for a moment.

"Yes, of course. You must be what? Five or six months by now?"

"No, no, not that far along," I said. Truthfully I had lost track.

"Well, I am glad to see you are going through with this. You were not so sure on the train. You are making the right decision. All life is precious. Sacred."

I nodded in agreement. "Can I ask you a question, Father?"

"Sure, anything you want," he said.

"Do you think angels are real and that they come down to earth?"

He paused to reflect. "I do believe in angels, yes. They are real," he said. "There is actually a Scripture that talks about them. . . .'"

His voice trailed off as he got up and walked over to the table to pick up his Bible. He flipped through the tattered leather book, the pages thin as tissue.

"Here it is," he said. "Hebrews 13. 'Do not forget to entertain strangers, for by so doing some people have entertained angels without knowing it.' There it is," he said.

My eyes widened. I had not heard that verse before. "Can angels come in any human form? Even an old lady?" I asked.

"Well, certainly. An old woman, a homeless man, a child, we never know. That is why it is so important to show the love of God to all we meet."

"I met a woman today. . .in your church. Did you see her, in the blue?" I asked.

Father Charlie knitted his eyebrows together. "Hmm. I don't recall. Did she sit with you?"

"No, she was up in front. I met her after the mass."

"And you think that maybe she was an angel?"

My face turned crimson. To hear it out loud sounded silly. "Well. . .I'm not sure, but I have never met anyone like her."

"Nothing is impossible with God," said Father Charlie.

"She spoke in a strange language over me. I am not sure what she was saying."

Father Charlie thought for a moment. "Have you ever heard of the gift of tongues? Some people have that gift, and God gives them revelation and knowledge not visible to the human eye."

My face lit up like a light. "That must be it," I said. "She knew about me, without knowing me. It was strange."

"Our God does work in mysterious ways," he said.

Father Charlie finished his tea and got up again. He went over to the table and grabbed an envelope. "More tea?"

"No, I will have to be going soon."

He handed me the manila envelope. "Here," he said. "Just a little something to help you on your journey."

I opened the envelope and found four crisp one-hundred-dollar bills. "Oh, my gosh," I said.

He just smiled. "It is not much, but I know you are struggling right now. Whatever I can do to help, I want you to know I am here for you. Please, please call me or come see me again."

Tears blurred my vision. "Thank you so much. I don't deserve this, but thank you."

"Ahh, none of us deserves anything. That is why they call it a gift."

Before I stood to leave he came near my chair, laid his hand on my head, and recited a prayer. "May the Lord bless you and keep you; the Lord make his face shine upon you and be gracious to you; the Lord turn his face toward you and give you peace."

My tears would not stop. I felt like my heart was breaking. I couldn't understand how I deserved this, but I was so grateful for the gift.

CHAPTER 10

Sheila was convinced God had sent me an angel. As she listened to my story, she kept crossing herself and chanting, "Jesus, Mary, and Joseph," over and over again. She told me it was a sign. A sign that this baby was God's will. I still was not sure about that, but my faith had been awakened.

I was beginning my fifth month, and for some reason I felt lighter. My legs were not as heavy, and I had a sensation of peace I could not pinpoint. As my belly ballooned, my bank account deflated. I worried about money and bills and what would happen when I could no longer work. I hid the envelope Father Charlie gave me in an old book on the top shelf of my bookcase. I knew I would need it sooner rather than later, but I wanted to conserve my resources.

Everyone at the agency was supportive, even Wendy. She finally recognized my baby bump. It only took her five-and-a-half months. But still she was being kind in her own way, looking the other way when I came in late. I felt new energy and hope for the first time in months. Even Jason noticed my new demeanor as I waddled past his cube.

"Hey, preggy," he called out. I didn't mind my new nickname, as long as he said it with a grin. Jason's sense of humor sustained me through some rough days. His gift was paying off. He had secured some gigs at a couple of downtown comedy clubs. I was dying to see his act, but by the time nine o'clock rolled around I was done. All I wanted to do was sink into my couch with a quart of jamocha almond fudge in my lap. The baby seemed to like it, too. Every spoonful elicited rapid little movements in my belly. For the first time in twenty-five years I did not worry about my weight. I was supposed to be gaining, especially since I lost eight pounds in the first trimester.

"Have a seat," said Jason. "How's the little guy?"

We both thought it may be a boy, especially now, after the strong internal kicks.

"He's a movin' and a shakin' in there," I said. "I think he will be good at soccer."

"Can I cop a feel?" he asked.

I blushed. "Okay, I guess."

I let Jason feel my belly. He loved it when the baby kicked. Sometimes he'd throw his nerf ball at my belly and yell, "Catch!" I would grab the ball and throw it back in his face.

"So have you given my offer any more thought?" he asked.

Looking him directly in the eye, I said, "Are you sure about this?"

"If I wasn't sure, I wouldn't have offered," he said, spinning around in his desk chair.

"Well, if you are really okay with all of this, then, yes, I guess."

"Yes! It will be awesome. No girl should have to do this alone. Plus, it will give me some new material for my stand-up act," he said.

"Hey! That's not fair! You can't use me like that. I thought you were doing this because you cared."

"You know I do, girl, but when opportunity arises—"

"Be nice. I will let you do this on one condition," I said.

"What's that?"

"That you promise not to make any jokes during the labor. Afterward, but not during. You need to be serious."

"Hmm." He tilted his head back, like he was in deep thought. "Not sure I can be serious, preggy. Jokes are my thing."

"No jokes," I said.

"They might just help you relax."

"Jason! I mean it, no jokes!"

"Okay, okay, I'll refrain. But can I bring my camera?" he asked.

"No! Absolutely not! There'll be no photos until after the birth—you got that?"

Jason smiled. "Yes, dear, I hear you. So when is our first Lamaze class?"

"Friday night. Seven o'clock."

"What do I wear to this party?"

"Just normal clothes. Something comfortable."

"Alright. Anything else I need to bring? Some light refreshments, a cool drink?"

"Jason, this is not cocktail hour. It's Lamaze."

"Oh, yes," he said as he started to mimic the instructor. "Breathe in through the nose, now out through the nose." He sat tall and did his best breathing for me.

"Hey, you're pretty good at this. Maybe we should trade places, and you can have this baby."

"I wish I could. You know if I could even take away one ounce of your pain, I would do it," he said, now more serious.

It was rare to see Jason use a serious tone, but when he did I listened.

"Thanks, J. I know you would."

Back in my own cube, I canvassed my desktop, sighing at all my unfinished work. The message light on my phone was blinking. Lifting the receiver, I punched in my code.

"You have two new messages," said the computerized voice.

"Hi, Grace, it's Father Charlie. Just checkin' in with you. Give me a call at the church. I have a question for you. Hope to hear from you soon." Beep.

Message two played. "This is Glenda. Calling to confirm your spot in my class this Friday night. We start seven sharp. Please bring water and a pillow." Beep.

Taking this class made me feel nervous. It made giving birth seem so real, and I wasn't ready for the class or the birth. I brought my mind back to Father Charlie and scribbled his number on my yellow legal pad. I doodled squares around the phone number, one on top of another. My mind was far away, and I felt powerless to coax it back to the present. *I'll just rest my eyes a minute and then get my reports done*, I told myself. Soon my mind drifted back to the sea. To the night I stayed on the beach. I dropped my pen, shut my eyes, and surrendered to the memory.

I slept with my head on Lee's chest. There was a soft knock on the bedroom window. It gradually got louder. Lee must have heard it, too. Thinking I was still asleep, he tried to move my head off his chest and roll me to the side of the bed. My eyes opened. For a second I couldn't remember where I was. My eyes took a mental inventory around the room. King-size waterbed, tall oak chest, guitar propped up against a bike near the closet door. Two surfboards hung on the opposite wall. I blinked a couple of times trying to wake up. Lee was already moving, making waves in the bed.

"Where are you going?" I asked.

"Shh, shh, go back to sleep," he said. He rubbed my head like I was a child. "I'll be back in a minute."

I looked toward the window where I heard the knocking. No one was there. Maybe I dreamed it. I rolled over and grabbed a pillow, hugging it close to my body. I wondered where he was going and who was at the window. Deep down, I knew the answer.

A few minutes later I heard the crash of glass. It came from the front room. I jumped out of bed, wearing only a T-shirt, and went to investigate. I could hear voices once I stopped in the hall.

"Angela! What are you doing?" yelled Lee. "Climbing through my window? Are you out of your mind?"

Angela broke the lamp as she fell through the window. All she cared about was finding me. "Where is she, Lee? I know she is in here!" she screamed.

Lee led Angela outside to the front porch. I heard the screen door slam. I jumped and turned and went back to the bedroom. One punch from Angela and I'd be on the floor. She was obsessed with Lee, but he insisted they were just friends. He wasn't attracted to her in *that* way. But she wanted to be more than friends. Why he put up with her obsession was beyond me. Maybe he liked it. I started to feel jealous. *Maybe he is not telling me the whole story.*

For the first month I knew Lee, we were just friends. I'd come up to the beach for the weekend to get out of the city. I'd lie in the sun while he surfed. At night we would hang out with George and his other friends and party. We didn't even have our first kiss until my fourth weekend. We were lying side-by-side, swinging in a hammock in George's front room. I remembered him holding my hand and leaning in for the kiss. It was soft, gentle and slow. And from that second I was hooked. I had spent almost every weekend up at his beach house. We never went too much further than kissing because Lee was usually stoned and would fall asleep. Until this visit, nothing more physical had happened.

I waited alone in the dark room. What was taking so long? I marched back out into the hall, determined to claim my man. I took a deep breath and pushed open the screen door. Lee was sitting on the step alone. He looked like a confused little boy. He heard me walk up behind him, but he didn't bother to look up. He just stared at the ground.

"I really hurt her," he said. I stood behind him but kept silent. I hoped he would explain more. He buried his face in his hands and mumbled, "What am I doing?" he said to himself.

I stood there not knowing what to say.

Finally he looked at me. "I'm sorry," he said. "She's crazy. And she's in love with me."

I crossed my arms in front of my chest. "What is actually going on, Lee?" I asked. "I thought you were just friends."

"We are, we are," he protested. "But I like her. I like talking to her, but that's all. There is nothing physical. But she wants more—she wants me."

I raised my hand in the air, signaling for him to stop. "I don't care what Angela wants," I said. "I care what you want. Who do you want?"

Lee hesitated. But then he turned and looked up at me. "I want you, babe, just you."

I wasn't sure I believed him. And I couldn't believe I was competing for his affection with a mean, fat, crazy woman. *What did she have that I didn't?* I couldn't lose Lee to her. Not to her. "You need to choose, Lee."

"I know—I'm sorry. She won't come back. Come here, babe," he said, reaching his arms toward me. I softened some and let him hold my hand. "I'm not going anywhere, okay?"

His words were what I wanted to hear, but the look in his eyes only made me doubt.

"Gracie, Gracie, wake up." I felt a hand grip my shoulder. "Gracie," the soft voice said again. It was Margo. She worked in the cube adjacent to mine. I jumped in my chair, startled back to reality.

"Are you okay?" she asked me.

"Yeah, I'm fine. Just exhausted. How long was I out?" I asked.

"I don't know. Maybe half an hour. You were awake when I left for my meeting. Good thing I came back early. Wendy's on her way," she said.

Wendy. I turned to my computer. I was supposed to have the schedules ready by four. She would be mad.

"I'm worried about you, Gracie," said Margo. "This is the second time this week you've fallen asleep at your desk. Is that normal? I mean in your state?" She nodded toward my body.

Margo was sweet. A little worrywart, but kind. Like me, she had relocated from the Midwest after college. She was younger, maybe twenty-two. This was her first job. She wore her sand-colored hair slicked back in a ponytail and only used a hint of lip gloss for makeup. Her green eyes were big and round. Her daily uniform was a crisp blouse tucked into a knee-length pencil skirt. Her two-inch pumps always matched the color of her skirt. She had the same shoes in four different colors.

Margo was smart in the office but didn't know much about life. She darted around my pregnancy at first. She ignored my weight gain. But when denial no longer worked, she referred to the baby as my "condition." To me, it sounded like I had some old-lady disease.

"You should not be out in your condition," was her favorite phrase. She meant well, but her controlled persona kept her at a safe distance. Anything messy, out of order, or too real sent her pumps pounding for the safety of her own confining cubicle.

"Margo, it's completely normal for a woman to be tired when she's carrying another life inside her all day long," I said.

At the word "life" she squirmed.

"What?" I asked.

"Well, it's not a life yet. It's just a mass of tissue," she said.

"Yeah, I used to think that too, but it's not," I said. "Like a big wad of Kleenex stuffed inside me?"

"No, not that kind of tissue. I mean just cells and stuff," she said.

"Oh. Cells and stuff," I repeated. "Let me ask you this: Are cells living?"

She glared at me. "Well, some are. But until it is born and takes a breath it's not fully alive. It's not a person."

"You try telling that to this little 'cell' inside me, who kicks me at least ten times a day and has a heartbeat."

"You can't hear the heartbeat," she said. "It's probably just your own. And in your condition you are not thinking clearly. I'm sure it doesn't have feet yet to kick."

I reached over and grabbed her perfectly manicured hand and placed it on my belly. Silently I pleaded with the life inside me to give her a sign, proof of its existence.

Margo was horrified. She pulled her hand away. "I don't want any part of this. This is your drama, your choice. Not mine. I hear Wendy. You better get your schedules done."

And then she stomped away.

That was the first time I ever saw Margo lose her cool. She never rocked the boat. Her perfect little shell just cracked, and it made me smile.

My feet hit the pavement on Madison Avenue. I walked briskly, in step with hundreds of commuters en route to Grand Central. In the mass of strangers I felt free. Free from judgment, shame and ridicule. No one knew my name. Or my story. I could be who they wanted me to be. A bearded man with a briefcase in hand held open a door for me.

"Thank you," I said.

I entered the station—a sea of navy-and-tan trench coats, all creating their own paths to their respective trains. I made my way to Track 37. The north line headed to the Bronx. I settled into the first empty seat and gazed out the window as the bodies rushed in all different directions. I spotted another "preggo" coming through the crowd. She looked weary after a day's work. My mind revisited the conversation with Margo. *A mass of tissue,* I said to myself. How could she be so naïve? But I thought the same thing the day I hopped up onto that examination table. I wondered if I would have gone through with it if the doctor hadn't shown me the heartbeat. The thought sent a chill down my spine.

"I know you are alive and well, little one," I said to my belly. "Margo must have flunked biology," I joked. "She didn't believe you were alive yet. What do you think about that?"

The tissue inside answered with a quick jab to my ribs. He was alive and kickin'.

CHAPTER 11

I fought to keep my eyes open as the train rattled down the track. My mind traveled back to the beach, as if to pick up where it left off in my previous dream.

I stood in cutoff jean shorts on Lee's porch. My skin was as brown as a berry. My curls danced in the wind, and I felt free, like a child.

Lee's friend George and his two kids rode up the street on their bikes. Lee opened the screen door and stepped onto the porch. He saw George and the kids.

"Go inside. Let me talk to George alone. Then we can talk," he said.

I hesitated. I liked George, and I didn't want to go inside. Lee looked at me. "Okay," I said as I slammed the screen door and walked inside the house.

Twenty minutes went by, and Lee was still talking to George. My patience was fading. I grabbed my suit and towel and headed out back to the beach house. The sun was hot, and I felt the rays burning my shoulders. I pulled open the wooden door, and it squeaked. Reaching inside the curtain, I turned on tepid water for my shower. I slid off Lee's T-shirt and held it in my hands. I paused, inhaling his scent, wishing he were mine. Tears ran down my face and landed on the soft cotton.

Why doesn't he love me? I wondered. *What is wrong with me?*

I stepped into the shower to drown out the questions in my head. Running my fingers through my tangled hair, I closed my eyes and tried to wash away my ugliness. The water-worn wood on the door creaked. My eyes opened wide. I lifted the shower curtain back and was startled to see Lee. He was just as startled to see me. He stood there, staring at me. I felt more naked than I was. It felt like he could see into my soul. He nodded, as if to ask permission. I didn't object. His strong hands peeled off his wet suit, and in seconds he was sharing my private shower.

I let him kiss me. I let him do other things I never let him do before. I let myself fall into the desire of the moment, making believe it was love.

An alarm went off inside me. "Wait, stop," I said.

Lee stopped for a moment and waited for me to speak.

"We don't have, I mean, I don't have. . .anything."

He knew I was not on birth control. "Don't worry," he said. "I'll be careful. It'll be okay."

If I do this for him, then he will love me. Everything will be okay. I coaxed my mind to believe this lie and surrendered into his arms.

A few minutes went by, and he stopped. I wasn't sure if he was done. He looked down and sheepishly said, "I'm sorry."

I was confused. *Sorry for what?*

He stepped out of the shower and pulled on his wet suit. I heard him zip it up. I stood alone in the shower. The door creaked open. "Stay as long as you like," he yelled as he left. "I have to meet

George. See you later." Those were his last words to me before he vanished to the sea.

I stood alone in the wooden shower house. My brain quickly registered that his plan to "be careful" didn't work. I felt more alone now than I did before I met him. I stayed in the shower and scrubbed my body again. My hot tears blended with the water that was now turning cold. I stepped out, grabbed my towel, and blotted my shaking body. I shimmied into my suit and pulled on my shorts. I left the T-shirt in a ball on the sandy floor.

I walked in a fog of denial to the beach. Maybe Lee would be waiting. He would come find me and take me to lunch. I would wait. This couldn't be it. This was not how I thought my love story would feel. It couldn't end this way.

Jab. I felt a sharp pain in my rib cage. The baby's kick jolted me back into the real world. It was stronger than normal. I squinted in pain and slowly straightened up in my seat. Another jab, sharp, to my left side. I froze in pain, hand to my belly. The woman sitting across the aisle looked over with concern in her eyes, but she didn't say a word.

I glanced her way, giving her a half smile, and then sank back into my seat closing my eyes. Not wanting to fall asleep and relive any more scenes from the past, I forced my mind to focus on the present. I mentally went over my checkbook register, trying to calculate my balance. Realizing I was on the border of the red zone, I shifted gears to avoid my financial woes. I reached into my bag to find my book of baby names. I used the time during my commute to narrow down my name selections. On the girl side,

Rebecca and Rosalie were at the top of my list. But I didn't feel one hundred percent sure about either choice.

A lot of thought should go into a name. That's what Father Charlie had told me. The meaning, the origin, and the sound it makes when you call him for dinner. These were all important details I must consider. I thumbed through the book I had already devoured several times. My finger stopped in the Ks. Katherine, Kate, Kay. These are all names listed under Katherine. Then there was Kayla.

The name rang a bell. *Where have I heard that name?* Oh, yeah, it's the name of a famous soap character from *Days of Our Lives.* I remembered meeting my girlfriends between classes to cram into the student center and watch the endless saga of Luke and Laura.

I longed for the carefree days of college when my biggest worry was missing *Days.* Kayla was Luke's sister. I couldn't remember the details, but I knew she was beautiful and smart. I said the name out loud: "Kayla." I liked how it sounded. Sweet and simple. "The origin is Greek," I read, "and the name means 'pure one.'" *How perfect for a baby*, I thought. I printed the letters, adding it to the girl's side on my list. I moved on to the boy names. Jacob, Matthew, Ryan, Noah. It was so hard to choose. I wished Lee were here. He would help me choose.

As my pregnancy had progressed, I heard less and less from Lee. He rarely returned my phone calls. I imagined that by a miracle of God he would have an awakening and realize I was the best thing that ever happened to him. He would bike to the station, stopping only to buy roses. He'd run up three flights of stairs to my apartment in the Bronx. Out of breath, standing at my door, he would ring my buzzer. I would waddle to the door, peek through the peephole. Only the roses would block my vision. With care

I would open the door, smiling at the sight of the flowers. Lee would drop to one knee, and barely breathing he would say, "I am so sorry. I've been a jerk. I love you more than any other woman. I want to be with you forever and take care of you and our baby. Please, give me a second chance. I won't let you down. I love you. Will you marry me?"

Of course I would forgive him, accept the roses and the proposal. I would move to Long Island, and we would have the cutest little family on the beach. *In your dreams,* I said to myself. That was all it was, a pitiful dream. I shook my head, trying to knock some sense into myself. Lee was avoiding me. I had to face reality and accept that he would not be there for me. I knew I would not be getting my fairy-tale ending. No, only the good girls got those. And I was no Snow White.

CHAPTER 12

Friday finally arrived. I inhaled deeply at the bottom of the subway stairs. The sun's light penetrated the city's haze and revived me, giving me the strength I needed to climb up to the street. I walked toward Park Avenue. I was eager to meet Jason and hoped he had not beaten me there. I was running a few minutes late, but knowing me well, Jason would surely wait.

I pulled out the yellow lined paper from my bag and found the address: 29 Park Avenue. The street was long and narrow framed on both sides with brownstones. It didn't seem to fit Glenda, my free-spirited Lamaze instructor. I imagined her living in the West Village, surrounded by loud artists and roaming cats. The Upper East Side was so rich and classy. Coco Chanel suits coupled with Manolo Blahnik heels—two things I was currently lacking.

I imagined the lives of the women living in these buildings. Doormen greeted them kindly as they began their day: "Good morning, ma'am." As they arrived home after a day at the spa and Fifth Avenue shopping, the same doormen hailed them cabs to meet their wealthy husbands for martinis and then dinner at Lusardi's.

Waddling down the sidewalk in my running shoes and teal coat, buttons bursting, I felt like a misfit toy in the land of the Upper East Side.

Jason's call broke my self-conscious stupor. "Hey, preggy, wait up!" He jogged down Park trying to catch up with me.

"Hey, I thought you'd beat me here for sure. Glad I didn't make you wait."

"Actually I've been running this block for thirty minutes looking for you," he said with a smile. "I wondered if I had the right address. You sure she lives in this neighborhood?"

"Yes, 29 Park Avenue—that's the address my midwife gave me. Kim highly recommended her. It has to be right."

Sensing my fatigue and frustration, Jason grabbed my hand as we walked the last few blocks. We stopped in front of a five-story brownstone with shiny gold numbers, confirming our destination.

"29 Park," said Jason. "You were right, preggo. You ready?"

Jason stared at me as I stood paralyzed, not able to speak or move. I was a long way from ready.

"Come on, preggy," said Jason. "It'll be okay."

"This makes it all so real. I don't think I'm ready. Are you sure *you* want to do this?" I asked him.

"Yes, of course, I've been needing some new material for my act," he said with a grin.

I was outraged. "Your act! You can't use me in your act. I'll be mortified."

Jason laughed and pushed me toward the door.

On weekends Jason did a thirty-minute bit down at the Comedy Cellar on McDougal. Just the image of us walking hand-in-hand would be worth the price of admission. Not only was I two inches taller than Jason, I outweighed him by at least sixty pounds. His wiry frame disappeared behind my round silhouette.

Jason pushed me up the stone steps, and we entered the building single file. A polite doorman led us to the foyer and offered to push the elevator button for us. "What floor?" he asked in an Italian accent.

"Five," I said.

"Five it is." He pushed the gold button and stood back.

"Think we'll both fit?" Jason joked.

"I don't know," I quipped back at him. "We might get stuck between floors."

Jason stepped in and squeezed my hand. We landed safely on the fifth floor, and the doors slid open. Hand-in-hand we walked to apartment 509.

A willowy woman opened the door and greeted us with a slow, quiet smile. She held the door open and motioned us inside. Her auburn hair flowed wild, just like her purple dress.

"Welcome," she finally said. "Please come in and join us. The others are waiting."

We followed her as she floated down a narrow hallway and passed through a door with hanging glass beads, made up of every color of the rainbow.

Jason shot me a look as we followed her through the beaded doorway. I pleaded with my eyes for him not to make a joke. He restrained himself but kept smiling like a goofy teenage boy. We entered a dimly lit room filled with women, each with a different size baby bump. All of them sat on the floor propped up by pillows. Their partners, I assume all husbands, sat behind them, assisting in the propping up. Their eyes were closed, and serene smiles calmed their faces.

I glanced at Jason's skinny frame. I might break him if we attempted such a position.

Glenda guided us to a floor pillow under a corner window. Jason helped me down in the most ungraceful manner. One woman opened an eye to see the commotion. I caught her staring. *Go back to your Zen state; it's just me, a big Oompa Loompa, trying to get down to my place on the pillows,* I said in my head.

Once I was safely down, planted on my pillow, I looked around for a place for Jason to sit. *Oh, no!* I panicked. *There's no room for him.*

Sensing my anxiety, Glenda gracefully moved an end table, making just enough room for Jason to squeeze in behind me. He sat down and whispered in my ear, "Don't sit back too far, preggy. You'll flatten me like a pancake."

I jabbed my elbow into his ribs, and he groaned out loud. This officially broke the Zen silence. Six pairs of eyes stared in our direction.

"Sorry, honey," I said with a fake smile.

Glenda beckoned the participants to give her their full attention. It was time to begin the breathing. She asked the husbands to wrap their arms around their wives' bodies and place their hands on their lovely brides' hearts. At this request my eyes widened. Not only had my belly grown to the size of an overripe watermelon, but my already D-cup breasts had grown to a letter of the alphabet I had never seen on those bras in Macy's. No way would Jason find my heart hidden under a swollen chest, heavily guarded by underwire.

He fumbled with his hands as he tried to perform the task like an obedient schoolboy. My cheeks flushed as I guided his hands down to my belly.

Glenda smiled. "Or you may place them on your lover's belly."

My ears perked up like a Golden Retriever seeing a squirrel. *Lover? There was no loving going on here. Just a good Samaritan coming to the aid of a husbandless harlot,* I thought.

Jason got a kick out of the "lover" language and quickly adopted it as his new term of endearment for me, replacing "preggo."

I closed my eyes and pretended to enter the Zen state. But I wanted to disappear from the planet. Glenda proceeded to lead the breathing. We imitated her and sounded like a nest of impatient snakes hissing, "Hee, hee, shee, sha," over and over again. It was quite exhausting, all that breathing. My head became light and dizzy. *This is not a normal way to breathe*, I thought.

After we hissed in unison for about thirty minutes, Glenda moved on to birthing positions. I never knew there was more than one. Apparently there were quite a few. She described each in detail: squatting, doggy style, sideways with your legs lifted and separated. It sounded more like the positions you get in to make the baby than to have the baby. But I listened, cocking my head, trying to imagine my body contorting into submission. Then she had the audacity to ask us to practice the positions—there, right then in that room full of strangers.

I heard Jason choke on his saliva at this request. The other couples moved in harmony, bending their beautiful bodies with grace into the requested positions. We sat there and stared like rude teenagers spying on their friends.

I looked back at Jason. He was staring at the buxom blonde next to us as she moved to all fours like a pregnant cat.

"Jason," I whispered. "Eyes up here," I said as I motioned to my face.

"Sorry," he said, looking back at me. "Which one do you want to try?" he asked.

"You're serious?"

"You heard the teacher. Which one, *lover?*" he said in a teasing whisper.

"Very funny," I said. I looked at the other women, trying to figure out what to do.

"Here, lay down on your side," said Jason. "I'll help you."

I fell to my side, and Jason sat next to me supporting my back. In that position I could see the faces of the couple sitting next to us. The husband was holding his wife in his strong arms and whispering in her ear, "I am here. We got this. You can do this, beautiful."

He rubbed her belly as he sat behind her, fully supporting her in every way.

She leaned back into his chest, all her weight bearing down on him. He didn't even flinch. His strength was sufficient to hold her.

My throat tightened as I tried to stifle my tears.

I would never have what that woman had. Jason was here for the moment, and I was grateful for that. But when the baby was born he'd go back to his life. I was alone. I had no strong man for me to lean on. No one to support me and love me.

I coughed out loud as my pain broke. My body trembled, and my salty tears soaked the shag carpet. Jason, unsure of what to do, lay behind me, spooning me with his hand on my shoulder. I curled into the fetal position and cried like a baby.

Glenda let us lie there as she and the other couples finished and exited into the hallway. Once the room was clear I found the strength to sit up. Jason sat and waited for me to speak first. I looked at him with smeared mascara covering my cheek. "Can we just go?" I pleaded.

"Sure, let's get outta here," he said.

He held my hand as I stood and braced my other hand on the end table. Glenda glided back into the room carrying a tray with a colorful teapot and two matching cups.

"I made you some Chamomile," she said. "It will calm your heart."

I tried to catch my breath. Jason nodded. "Thank you." He took the cup from Glenda and handed it to me.

"Here, take a sip," he said. "There's no rush."

I looked him straight in the eyes to thank him without words. I sipped my Chamomile.

"You know, sweetie, I also do private sessions. Maybe that would suit you better?" Glenda asked.

I already knew the answer, but I asked anyway. "How much are those?"

"Eighty-five a session or you can purchase seven for just five hundred," she said.

Just five hundred. That was my share of the rent. "Thank you, Glenda," I said politely. "I will think about it."

"Sure," she said, "you just let me know."

We both knew I was not coming back, not for a group session or a private.

I finished my tea in a serene state. I wrote out my check for forty dollars and handed it to her.

"It is so wonderful to know you," she said as we walked to the door. She clasped my hand between hers and held it in a prayer position. "If there is anything, anything at all I can do for you, please let me know."

"Thank you," I said. "I will."

Glenda freed my hand and then squeezed Jason's. "Take good care of this one."

Then she bowed her head, her hands pressed together in prayer, and whispered, "Shanti. Peace with you."

I mumbled "you too" and followed Jason out the door.

It felt good to step off Park Avenue on to Lex and leave the Upper East Side behind. Jason held my hand as we walked to the subway stop at 77th.

"Hey, preggy, you did great in there."

He leaned in to hug me, and I hugged him back. He patted my head. "Get home safe. I'll see ya Monday."

"Yeah, Monday," I said.

"Thank you!" I yelled as he was moving away from me. "Thanks for everything."

"No big deal. Go home. Rest."

He winked and walked away. Then he turned back. "Hey, can I use that side-squat position for my act Saturday?"

I finally cracked a smile. "Yeah, sure. Go for it. No way I'm using it. It's all yours."

He grinned a big goofy grin and called out one last time, "Later, lover."

"Later," I said as I descended the dark subway stairs.

CHAPTER 13

The Lamaze session had worn me out. It seemed like a lot of work, especially for a baby I wasn't even sure I was keeping.

How was I supposed to take care of a baby, alone, in New York City? I could barely take care of myself. Living paycheck to paycheck. I opened my checkbook, staring at the register. The balance was shrinking. I could have used that forty dollars for something important like food. What a waste. What was I thinking going to some upper eastside Lamaze group? I knew I would not be visiting Miss Glenda again, no matter how good she was claimed to be. I would just have to do this breathing and birthing on my own. I knew Jason had tried, but he was in uncharted waters. The closest thing he had known to being a birth cheerleader was coaching second base on our company softball team. I could picture him in the birthing room with me. Standing still, eyeing the scene, and then, without warning, he would yell, "Go! Go! Run! Now!" He'd force the baby out of me with his commands. "Come on, batter, batter, swing."

Now that was something he could use for his act. The imagery of it put me in a better mood for the moment. But the reality was that I was still alone. No husband. No partner, no daddy for my baby. How could I keep my baby and be a single mother?

Thank God the 4 train was only a few blocks from my apartment. I stood, exhausted, waiting for the train to come. Glancing at my watch, I silently chanted, "Please hurry, please hurry, please hurry," as if the engine could hear my plea. A few seconds later the train pulled up to the platform, and the doors slid open with a scratchy squeak.

With one long stride I stepped off the platform and into the train. It smelled worse than usual. I plopped down in the first vacant seat. It was empty for a Friday night. Not too many people heading into the city. It was still early. I knew the train would be standing room only by eleven o'clock. People returning home, still buzzed from Friday night's happy hour.

The train swayed and jogged down the track, soon to plunge deep into the underground city. Darkness enveloped me as I sat swaying side-to-side, letting the train rock me into a trance-like state. Every few minutes flashes of light would dart through the stained window, teasing me with their dance. But the light always vanished and left me sitting alone in dark.

"175th Street!" announced the conductor. The train jerked to a stop, and the bell rang, signaling the sliding of the doors. An old woman got on, her skin dark and worn like my favorite leather gloves. My gloves were still soft to the touch as I imagined her skin was. Her right hand tightly clasped the hand of a small boy, pulling him off the platform. They sat two rows down from me, finding their seat quickly. She whispered something into the little boy's ear then let go of his hand. Her tapestry bag perched on her lap blocked my view of the boy.

I glanced at them every few minutes, curious about their destination. The woman looked straight ahead, eyes fixed on the ads plastered to the train walls.

I noticed a high-top sneaker kick out from the woman's large frame. Then a little round head bobbed forward, peeking at me from behind the woman's bag. His eyes were dark like chocolate.

Catching my glance, he got scared and sat back in his seat. I looked away, giving him some space. Three minutes later he leaned forward to take another look at me. This time he stared a little longer. He continued this game of hide-and-seek with me for the next fifteen minutes. With each lean he became braver and held his gaze a little longer. I leaned forward, exaggerating my movement. I gave him a closed-lip smile and leaned back. Oblivious to our little game, or choosing to ignore it, the woman sat motionless.

We played in silence, peeking and hiding. Soon a smile lit up his face. The innocence of him, sitting there smiling at me, playing this game with a stranger on the subway, completely took me over.

He was trusting, vulnerable. A joyful child playing in the moment. That child-like quality overwhelmed me with its purity. I gasped for air as I choked on my own saliva. This startled him, and he crinkled his forehead. I blinked away the water pooling in my eyes and gave him a reassuring smile.

"120th!" yelled the conductor. I jerked in my seat as the train headed into the station. The woman grabbed the boy's hand while still clutching her bag to her breast. The train jolted backward before coming to a complete stop. The woman, now standing, let go of the boy to grab the silver metal pole. The little boy had squeezed behind her and was holding on to the hem of her coat. His eyes were glued to mine.

The woman found her balance and stepped across the train to the open sliding door next to my seat. She muttered something to him in what sounded like French. He followed behind her gripping her coat in one hand. As they stepped by me, his free hand grazed my arm and rested a moment on my bare hand. He looked up at my eyes for some sign of approval. I smiled big, wanting to pick him up in my arms. He smiled back, showing all his teeth. He squeezed my pinkie finger and in an instant he was gone. I watched him leave as the doors slammed in my face.

Something in him broke through my heart. It was as if a spring was uncorked. By 72nd Street my face had been washed of its painted-on colors.

CHAPTER 14

Saturday morning finally arrived. No intruding alarm interrupted the peace of my sleep. No train to catch. No desk full of schedules. The only obligation I had was to meet with Father Charlie, but that wasn't until three. I was free. Or so I thought.

I ate a long leisurely breakfast of hot coffee—just one lingering cup—thick French toast layered with sliced strawberries, and a side of crunchy bacon. Nothing like eating for two. I stretched my stuffed body out on the couch and closed my eyes. In that space between consciousness and dreamland I rested, suspended in time.

I tried to imagine what this little person inside me looked like. Was she a girl, or was he a boy?

I hoped and prayed she or he would be okay. After I discovered I was pregnant, but before my visit to the Park Avenue doctor, I wasn't too sure what I would do. I thought I would get a quick procedure to end this unplanned interruption to my life, and then all would go back to normal. So I indulged in salty margaritas and even did shots of tequila with my friends. One late lonely night I took two hits of a joint that my friend's boyfriend offered me. I tried anything to escape the current circumstances and live in the fantasy land of *everything is all right* until the day of termination.

My agony, shame, and denial allowed me to believe the lies: It's not really a person until after twelve weeks. That's why doctors aren't allowed to do abortions past the twentieth week in most parts of the country. If it was legal, then it must be okay. It's only a bunch of cells anyway. A mass of tissue. No soul. No spirit. Not human. Not living. And with my party lifestyle it probably would be a mess anyway. Better to get rid of it. I would be doing it a favor by ending its existence now. It would never survive in this world. It would hate this world. This world would hate it. Maybe it would be missing toes or only have half a brain. How cruel would it be to bring a baby into the world with missing digits.

And even by the slightest chance, a miracle even, if it did survive and was normal, I'd be a terrible mom. I couldn't provide clothes and shoes, braces and college. Without college it would not become anything. The kid would be selling day-old hot dogs at a convenience store at two in the morning. That was no life.

Then there was the most obvious reason not to have this child: he wouldn't have a dad. If it was a girl, she would seek out the attention and affection of men at an early age. Have unprotected sex in high school and get pregnant. Then I would have to raise her child, too.

And if it was a boy? That would be a different nightmare. He would not know how to be a man. To do guy things. He would hate women. He could be a rapist or a serial killer. He would be mocked and beat up at school. He would be a sissy or a bully. He would never sell hot dogs at 7-Elevens—he would rob them.

My mind went frantic. Dark thoughts spun like horses on a carousel. As each horse circled by, they turned into babies. Each one looked at me, accusing me with pain-filled eyes asking, "Why?"

I tried to move, to escape this dream, but I was stuck in the middle, on top of the machinery that made the ride spin. Coarse leather straps were wrapped around my wrists, tethering me to the hard metal motor. On my ankles were heavy chains securing me to a pipe below. Each time I tried to run free, the chains yanked me back in place with an unforgiving force. The more I tried to set myself free, the more the chains would cut into my flesh. Blood covered my ankles and feet.

My hands were swollen and blood red. I was bound by a dark force that delighted in my pain. I could not get free.

Bound by terror and fear, I was stuck in the dark abyss.

In the far distance I could hear a shrill ring. It was repetitive and persistent. I must have heard it a hundred times before the tone was powerful enough to release me from my tormenting dream. Like a diver coming up for air, I sat up forcefully, gasping for my breath.

Eyes wide open. Hair plastered to my cheeks. Legs stuck to the couch, I sat still, listening to the ring of the telephone. I felt dizzy, like I was still on that merry-go-round of torture. The ringing stopped.

I looked around the room, checking to make sure I was home. I felt that my mind and body had been transported to another world—a dark one where bright painted horses turned into monsters and evil spirits delighted in my pain.

The winter air hit my cheeks like a cool kiss. I stood outside the courtyard and took in as much air as I could, filling my tight lungs. Their expansion gave me renewed energy to make the eight-block walk to St. Michael's where Father Charlie was waiting.

Painted bluejays flew as a flock over the steeple of the red church. I paused a moment to catch my breath and watch the birds in flight. The two front birds left the flock and circled back around, almost to say, "Hey, want to fly with us today?"

If only I could magically transform into a blue bird and fly far, far away. Above the chaos and clutter of the city. I yearned to be free from my condition, from the choice I was forced to make. Time was running out. My due date fast approaching. I had to decide.

Could I be a mother or not?

What was best for this little life growing inside me?

I watched the blue birds loop around the church and head west. They stayed together, forever loyal, never leaving the other's side.

I wished I had a partner, a friend to stay at my side. As they flew from my vision I exhaled my loneliness.

I paused at the top of the stone stairs, enjoying one more minute of sunshine.

Father Charlie must have sensed my presence because one of the carved doors swung open to escort me in. "Are you coming in?" he asked.

"Do I have a choice?"

"You always have a choice."

He was talking about more than just coming inside. I struggled to step by him, moving with the grace of a rhinoceros. I waited as he bolted the door, and then we walked down the long, dark church aisle.

His office was to the right and back of the altar, but you had to step up two red velvet stairs onto the altar. I hesitated as we approached. I felt unworthy to enter this sacred space, reserved for the holy ones: popes, priests, and praying people.

Everything was mysterious up on the top step. I had never been up farther than the first pew. Father Charlie was already across, standing at his secret door, as patient as a saint. "Come, Gracie," he said.

I tiptoed my way across the red velvet sea and managed to make it to the other side without being struck down by lightning. *Do they let unwed mothers on the altar?* I wondered.

"You made it," he said, trying to coax a smile.

I am sure I looked like a cow before the slaughter. But once he opened his private door I found refuge in an overstuffed paisley chair. Father Charlie sat behind an empty mahogany desk. The only items on it were a lamp and a Bible. The lamp provided the only light to the dim room, which was barren except for a small bookcase, a statue of some saint I'd never seen, and a basin with water. High on the wall, light peeked in through a stained-glass window, giving the room an amber glow. The wooden floor was so clean it shone like the moon.

Father Charlie's question broke the silence. "Have you made your decision to parent or give up your child for adoption?"

I could not answer. I shook my head no.

"You're still working?"

"Yes."

"Any word from the father?"

"No, no word."

"Have you thought about my offer?"

I had been staring at the small piece of stained glass as I answered his questions. But now my eyes met his.

"Offer?"

"Yes. To visit my family and meet Samantha. My parents would love to have you," he said. "I think it would be good for you to get out of the city for a few days. Help clear your mind."

"Are you sure they have room?"

"There's plenty of room in the country. A big empty house except for Sam and Ben. No one else is staying there. Even my old room is available."

"I guess it would be nice to get away."

"I think the time with Sam and Ben would help you with the choice you have to make."

"Yeah, I guess so. It's not an easy decision to make."

"No, it is not, my dear. But give yourself some credit. You already made the most difficult choice. You chose life for your child. It takes a lot of courage to walk in obedience. God sees that. He will honor that and walk with you through this valley," he said.

He could tell I did not believe what he was saying. My shame blocked any good words from reaching me.

"Gracie, keep choosing life. In everything acknowledge Him. He will guide your steps."

I desperately wanted to believe him. I stared at his face, trying to let the words sink in, but something was in the way. How could God still love me after all I had done wrong? Would He really lead me and guide me? And how would I know if it was Him? I couldn't hear Him. God felt so far away.

I didn't dare come too close to Him and have Him see me in this condition. He would be so disappointed. Even though I knew He already knew, I didn't want to rub it in His face. My head felt heavy from all this thinking. I just wanted to hide beneath the shiny floor boards.

Father Charlie stopped talking.

He looked at me as a father who watches his child board the school bus for the first time. Memories of Catholic school bus rides came to my mind. A child pleads with his eyes to his father. "Don't make me go!" But the father hands him his lunchbox, gives him a hug, and tells him to get on that bus. It is time. He must be brave. He tells his son, "Even though I will not be on the bus, I will be with you in your heart. And when you come back at the end of the day I will be waiting."

The child clings to his daddy, too afraid to climb aboard the yellow bus filled with strangers. But the father knows best. He releases his child's grip and tells him to go.

"I will be here," he says one last time.

So the child climbs the big steps, one at a time. Pausing after each step to see if his father is still watching. And he is. He runs to an empty seat in the back and presses his frightened face against the smeared glass window as the bus revs into gear. The father still stands. Even as the bus turns the corner and is out of sight, the father still stands on the curb. His presence is constant.

Father Charlie handed me an envelope. "You will need this to board the train," he said.

Next to the ticket was another one-hundred dollar bill. I could not reach out to take the envelope. He laid it on the table. I looked at it, feeling unworthy.

"Take it, Gracie. It's a gift."

That word again: *gift*. Why was it so hard to receive? I felt as if I needed to earn it.

"My dad will pick you up at the station. They are expecting you for dinner a week from Wednesday," he said. "Come on—it's time. Time to go. Get up now. Go in peace."

As I tried to speak, my voice broke. "Thank you," was all that came out, followed by a mournful cry.

Father Charlie stood and went to open the door. He gave me some time to pick up my broken pieces and meet him at the door.

In silence we crossed the red altar and walked single file down the dark aisle, Charlie leading me each step of the way. When we got to the heavy carved door, he opened it and waited. His eyes were full of love, and his voice was gentle.

"You go, my dear. Let us see where God leads you. I will be here when you get back. I will wait," he said.

CHAPTER 15

sat in my cubicle waiting for Wendy to return from lunch. I'd rehearsed the words in my head a thousand times. It was past two o'clock. What if today was one of the days she didn't come back after lunch?

I looked at my ticket. It was for Wednesday. I had to tell her today, or there would be no way I could go. I leaned back in my chair, closed my eyes, and chanted, "Please come back, please come quickly."

"Who are you talking to?" asked Margo.

Margo's voice broke my mantra. She had been avoiding me since our last conversation. I was surprised to see her in my cube.

"No one. Just waiting for Wendy to get back from lunch," I said.

"Oh. Well, you know, she went out with the boys from account services. They are probably having a liquid lunch at the company store," she said. "She could be awhile, if she even comes back at all."

"Yes, I know," I said. Margo had a knack for making things worse.

"Why do you want to see her so bad, anyway?"

"I need to talk to her."

Margo would not let it go. "About what?"

"How about it's none of your business," I said.

"Is it about the—." Her words stopped, and she just motioned with her head to my big baby belly.

I looked at her and waited. "Just say it, Margo," I said. "You can't say it, can you?"

"Yes, I can."

"Well, then, what is it? Say the word."

"Is it about the. . .baby?" she finally said.

"Wow. . .you actually called it a *baby*. I'm impressed," I said. She just stared at me like an ornery little sister.

"So why is it a baby now, Margo?" I asked.

"I've been reading up on it, you know. I'm not stupid."

"Well, that's good to know," I said with a smirk.

I wanted to find out exactly what she was reading, but a loud burst of laughter stole my attention. It was Wendy and her gang of cohorts.

"Excuse me, Margo, but I need to go see Wendy."

"Well, good luck talking to her now. She's wasted," Margo added.

"Yes, I know." I pushed past Margo and cut off Wendy as she teetered to her office.

"Wendy, can I talk with you a minute?"

"Sure, come on in. Have a seat. Take a load off," she said with a slur.

I sat down. Wendy staggered to her side of the desk and plopped in her leather chair. She stared at me for a second, her smile turning to disgust.

"Wow, girl! How far along are you now? You are huge!"

"I'm glad you noticed. Yes, I'm at the end of my fifth month, almost halfway there. Yippee for me!" I raised my arm up and shook my hand in the air. Her glassy eyes just stared at my belly.

She looked confused. Wendy reached for her glasses and put them on her head crooked.

"May 10 is my due date," I said.

"Time does fly when you're havin' fun!"

I couldn't believe she just said that. This had been the longest five months of my life. And I would not call any of it fun. I wanted to shake her skinny, staggering body.

"Well, yes, but that's not why I'm here. I need to ask you something."

"What are you waiting for?" she said. "Ask already."

"I know I have gone over my allotment of sick days, with the pregnancy and morning sickness. And I have been late a little more than usual, but I still do have a little time from the Netter project, so I was wondering if I could take a little time off next week to go to the country?" Before she could answer, I added, "It's just three days. I'll leave Wednesday and be back by Monday."

As I recited my monologue, Wendy searched her desk drawer for some treasure, and I was not even sure she heard me.

"You got any Altoids?" she asked me. "I bought a new tin yesterday, and for the life of me I don't know where I put them."

"They're behind your phone," I said. "Here," and I handed them to her.

"Oh, yes! There they are! I knew I put them somewhere," she said.

She dumped two mints into her lipstick-stained mouth. "Now where were we?"

Oh, no. Did she not hear a word I said? Did I have to say it again?

"Time off. I need a few days off next week," I said.

"Oh, yes, yes. Sick days, yes. Take as many as you need. That morning sickness must be getting worse. Just fill out a time form and leave it on my desk. I have to leave early today," she said. Her phone beeped, and she shooed me out of her office so she could take the call.

Margo was standing outside our cubes waiting for me to return. Her arms were crossed and her head tilted to the side, like the mom of a teen late for curfew.

"By the look on your face, I guess your talk with Wendy went well," she said.

"Yes, it did," I said. "I'm going to the country. And I'm not going to miss this place one little bit."

"So who is in the country?" she asked. "The daddy?"

That was the first time she ever mentioned the father. We never talked about personal stuff. Only work.

"No. . .he's not there."

"So are you keeping it?"

"By *it* do you mean the baby?"

"What else would I mean?"

"Just checking," I said. "So what did you find in your research?"

"I told you. Just some articles, stories and stuff. So are you?"

"I don't know yet. That's why I'm getting out of here for a while. Clear my head."

"Well, good luck with all that."

"Okay," I said.

I buttoned up my long coat and got my things to leave. I looked back at Margo. She looked sad, like she had just lost a friend.

CHAPTER 16

I stood waiting for the elevator. The red numbers lit up one at a time signaling the descent: 29, 28, 27. I was irritated it was taking so long to come down. The elevator appeared to be stuck on floor 21. I closed my eyes, hoping that if I kept them shut long enough floor 17 would illuminate.

Ding! The rumbling of hydraulics startled me. The doors finally opened, and three men in black suits exited in haste. I stepped back and let them pass. The others stared at my body as I awkwardly stepped into the padded box. My eyes focused on the specks in the tile floor. I tried to hide in the back corner. A tall woman who looked like a Vogue model stood next to me. Her hair was slicked back into a high ponytail. She stared at the numbers. Two men stood to the right of me, one bobbing up and down to the tunes blaring through his head phones. The other checking out the tall blonde. Each totally engrossed in their own small worlds, oblivious to my presence in their personal space.

We descended to the fifth floor, and the doors slid open. Finally a connection was made. Jason's eyes found mine like a nail to a magnet. An invisible beam of energy connected us even though he was forced to stand in the opposite corner. Still, no one spoke. But Jason's presence brought hope into those lonely walls, and I felt grateful.

We hit the ground floor. People got into position, buttoning top buttons, grasping handbags tightly and finding sunglasses. They were like runners setting up in the wooden starting blocks before the hundred-yard dash. Ready, set, go! As the bell rang, doors opened, and they were off. Bodies merged in all directions entering the flow of people eager to leave the world of spreadsheets and cubicles and enter the train stations and cabs, whisking them off to their weekends.

I stepped off to the side to wait for Jason. The salty scent of pretzels drew me toward the vendor on the street. Surely he would find me here. Just a quick snack to tide me over.

"Hey, preggo!" he said when he found me. "I knew you'd go for the pretzel man!" He laughed.

"Want one?" I asked. "They're yummy."

"No, don't want to spoil my dinner. But you enjoy."

Jason grabbed my hand and led me through the maze of suited people. We stopped at a hot dog stand.

He glanced at me. "Mustard? Right?"

He already knew the answer, but he was smart to ask. Lately my taste buds were playing tricks on me, making me despise foods I normally loved and crave food that used to repulse me.

"I thought you didn't want to spoil your dinner," I asked with a grin.

"This is just the appetizer, lover," he said.

Jason paid the hotdog vendor, and we made our way to the cement steps of the library. "So you have big plans for the weekend?"

My eyebrows lifted.

"Really? You are asking me my plans?" I said. "Well, if you must know, I have a hot date with this guy I met on the phone.

He's taking me to a Broadway show. I neglected to mention my current state. Do you think he'll notice?" I looked at Jason with my best baby doe eyes. He played along.

"Nah, wear something black and baggy. He'll think you ate too many slices at lunch." He said.

I punched him in the arm. "Very funny," I said. But that sounded good. "You wanna go to Ray's and get a slice?"

"You're not even done with your hot dog, and you want a slice!" said Jason.

"Yes, I want a slice! A big one."

"You need to eat more healthy, preggo," he said. "No more junk food for you. What you need is some good protein."

"I made a steak the other night."

"Well, that's more like it."

"Yeah, it was so good. I cooked it so rare it was dripping with blood," I said.

Jason stopped eating mid-bite. "You're serious?"

"Oh, yes. It was a bloody steak. It had so much red juice that I drank it straight out of the pan."

"Girl, that's just gross. Please promise me you won't do that on your date tonight. He'll think you're a vampire," he joked.

"Ha, ha, funny. Like I'll ever have a date again in my life." No man would ever want me now. And what if I kept the baby? Who would date a single mom? It was a sure sign of solo Saturday nights. My hope of a romance and a husband dissolved as fast as the salt in my mouth.

"Now don't say that, Gracie. Look at me and Linda. She has three little rug rats, and I still love her," he said.

Jason had been dating Linda almost a year now. He would eventually marry her. And he would be a great dad to her kids.

"Yeah, but you're a rare bird," I said. "There are not many more like you. All the good ones are taken."

He smiled.

"Now, if you would just dump miss rosy cheeks and marry me, all would be right in the world," I said.

Jason smiled a sad smile. I could feel his compassion. I had known him for almost two years, but we were never an item. He wasn't my type. But I loved him like a brother. And I think he loved me, too. Like a little sister. I was glad Linda wasn't the jealous type and was cool about him helping me. Not many women would be.

"I'm pathetic, aren't I?" I asked.

Jason smiled at me. "No, I wouldn't call it that. You're just alone and pregnant."

We sat, finishing the last of our hot dogs.

"Have you heard from him?" he asked.

"No, nothing. I've tried to call him, but he won't answer. It's like he just vanished. He knows about the baby, but he doesn't care."

"Screw him!" he said. "You don't need him."

I didn't say anything. The thing was, I did need him. I desperately needed Lee to care, to love me, to do something, anything. But my gut told me that if I kept the baby to raise I would be doing it alone.

Jason placed his hand on my head and messed up my hair. "Well, I'm here. I will not leave you, preggo."

"I know," I said. "What would I do without you?"

"Oh, stop looking so sad, or I'll have to get you that rare juicy steak and heaven knows I couldn't stomach you drinking the blood."

"Don't tease me!" I said. "That sounds so good right now!"

"Go home and eat some ice cream like a normal pregnant woman."

"Normal?" I said. "You calling me normal?"

"Yeah, guess that's a mistake. You are far from normal."

"I'll take that as a compliment."

"You better," he said. Jason stood up and took our empty hot dog papers and put them in the trash. He came back and helped me up off the stairs. "You ready?"

"Yes. You need to get home to the wife and kids," I joked.

"Hey, now. She is not my wife yet," he said.

"I know. But she will be. You will do the right thing. You are one of the good guys."

Jason smirked. "Yeah, well, someone's gotta be."

We walked down to the street, and Jason hailed me a cab. He opened the door and helped me climb into the back seat.

"Get her home safe," he said to the driver as he handed him a wad of cash. "Be good, preggo," he said as he shut the door.

"'Bye, J."

The cabby took off into traffic, and I sat back battling my emotions. Sadness invaded my heart, and jealousy attacked my mind. Linda was lucky.

Anger came in and overtook jealousy. The anger pointed its ugly fat finger at me, saying, *"You sure know how to pick them! Why did you pick a guy like Lee, you stupid fool?"*

"I don't know," I said out loud. *I don't know.* Why did I? What was so broken in me that I chose one of the bad guys? I didn't have the answer to that.

I looked out the window, letting the anger go. Sadness came back. This was not the way it was supposed to be. I looked up to the sky, wondering if God could hear me now. If He could, I wanted some answers. What happened to me? Why did I feel so broken? But, most of all, where was *my* Jason?

The cabby interrupted my self-flogging. "Where to?"

"205th and Moshula Parkway," I answered.

"Can't take the Deegan. Everyone's trying to get out of the city. It's the weekend. Have to cut across town to Highway One. Hope you don't have plans tonight, cuz it's gonna be a long ride," the young driver said.

I closed my eyes, sank into the cracked vinyl seat, and held on for the ride.

CHAPTER 17

Glass shattered on the street outside my bedroom window. The sharp crash interrupted my slumber and woke me as adrenaline rushed through my body. I turned my head, stretching my neck to see the numbers on the clock. The green numbers glowed in the dark: 2:41 a.m.

I heard male voices outside the window, loud as thunder. I could feel the hostility in the air. I lay, still as a corpse, too afraid to get up and look. Out of the corner of my eye I saw a water bug as fat as a baby carrot. It crawled in slow motion across the neon number. Cockroaches and mice scurried in the walls making scratchy sounds.

I hated this apartment. But Michelle and I couldn't afford anything in the city. Our last apartment over the bar was crawling with even bigger rats, so this wasn't so bad. At least we had space. I only saw the roaches if I snuck up on them in the middle of the night.

When I came to the city to be with my first love, Patrick, I stayed with him a few months until I found a job and my own apartment in Queens. He lived in a penthouse apartment on the Upper East Side. Even his place had roaches. If I had to go into the kitchen at night for any reason I'd reach my arm out long, stand back, close my eyes, and then turn on the lights. I would wait at least thirty seconds until I knew they were all gone, back into their tiny hiding places. Seeing made them real. If I didn't see them, I could pretend they didn't exist.

In my room I lay still as a stone, listening to the brawl below. Eventually it would end. More glass shattered as a beer bottle was flung at a street light. In the Bronx a church or a pub stood on every corner. Tonight the pub hoppers were in full force. I waited in the dark, too afraid to move and hoping the fight would end soon. I rolled over to go back to sleep. In sleep I could live the life of my dreams, far away from the brawls and bugs.

But the drunks would not let me escape into slumber. Forced to get up, I rose from my futon and pulled on my wool socks. I slid on the hardwood floors over to the window to check out the damage. Broken glass blanketed the sidewalk and street creating a mosaic of green, brown, and red. Looking closer, I saw that the red was not just glass, but blood. Bottles were rolling in the street, and a cracked baseball bat lay in the middle. A beaten man sat on the curb, holding his head in his hands.

When we found our two-bedroom walk-up in the quiet Bronx neighborhood close to the Botanical Gardens, it felt like a peaceful Irish village. For the most part, the lads liked their drink, but they were too friendly to fight. As the days went by, gangs from the north and south started closing in on our little neighborhood, trying to claim new territory. I dared not enter certain parts of the Bronx, but the Parkway was pleasant. Those good Irish boys were just trying to fight for their turf. Why did the gangs have to invade our village? I wished they would go back to Fordham and leave us alone.

I heard keys jiggling in the lock to the front door. At first my heart skipped a beat. Michelle was staying with her boyfriend for the weekend. I listened with caution as the keys jiggled in the lock. After that break-in I never felt safe.

The lock released, and the door flung open. Thank God it was Michelle. I could let myself breathe again.

"Gracie, you in here?" she called.

Her heels click-clacked as she walked into the kitchen, dropped her keys, and opened the fridge. I heard a can open, and then she click-clacked her way to my room.

"Who you hiding from? The boogie man?" she asked when she saw me under my covers. "What, you having hot flashes now? It's colder than a witch's tit in here!" She came over to the futon, and I came up for air.

"Hey, it's you," I said.

"Who else would it be? You expecting company? I see you already have some," she said as her eyes spotted my water bug crawling along the heat register. We had hot water heat, and the bugs loved to lie there.

"You plan on keeping that guy?" She looked at the dead one by the window. Michelle could always make me laugh. No matter how dire the circumstance, she could make me smile.

"The heat isn't working again," I said. "I called the super last night."

"We need to get out of this hole. If that baby doesn't freeze to death, then those bugs will eat it!" she joked.

"A little extreme there," I said.

"Come on into my room. You can wrap up in my down comforter and sleep on a real bed. I'll call the stupor—I mean the *super*."

She dialed the number, but then I heard her hang the receiver back on the wall without saying anything.

"No answer," she said. "Figures. He's probably lying out on the sidewalk with that other bloke from the bar."

She came back into her room and sat down at her mirror to remove her makeup. "So have you heard from our friend Lee?"

"What do you think?"

"By the tone of your voice, that would be a no," she said. "He's a loser."

"So what does that make me?"

"A loser, too!" She laughed.

"Michelle, I'm not in the mood. But maybe you are right."

"Oh, you know I'm just messin' with you."

Michelle was not the mushy type. She used humor in almost every situation. This was all too much for her to deal with, but I knew she cared in her own way. She would tease me, but her actions spoke louder than her words.

"So you know what you are doing yet?"

"I think so, but not sure. I've already fallen in love with this little life, but I'm not sure I can do it alone," I said.

"You won't be alone," she said.

I just looked at her. She smiled as she patted on her face cream.

"You have those water bugs. They're not going anywhere by the looks of it."

"Very funny. I was too squeamish to kill them and throw them out. Have the super do it," I said. "If he ever calls back."

"Move your big belly over—I'm lying down."

CHAPTER 18

Wednesday finally arrived. I was eager to escape the city and find peace in the country. The air in the city was thick as gravy, and the sky was gray. I left work early and headed west toward Penn Station. Sixth Avenue was bustling with service trucks, cabs, and buses emitting clouds of smoke. My train departed at 4:10 on Track 17. It was empty and easy to find a vacant seat. I grabbed two toward the front and spread out, giving myself room to breathe. I craved the solitude of the three-hour ride upstate. I'd never been north of the Bronx and wondered what upstate New York looked like. People talked about mountains and forests. Since I grew up in Colorado, they must have meant hills. I had never heard of mountains in New York.

I tried to picture Father Charlie's parents. His dad was an attorney, and his mom was a housewife. Even though all the children were grown and raised, she continued to stay home and keep up the house. Samantha, his sister, had recently come back home. Sam, as he called her, graduated from Notre Dame—the home of the famous fighting Irish. She got pregnant her junior year and ended up keeping her baby boy. The father wasn't in the picture, so she went back home to live with her mom and dad. I admired her and was a little nervous to meet her. I couldn't imagine how hard it must have been to raise a baby alone.

I wonder what my parents would do. I'd been too afraid of their disapproval to tell them the news. Two thousand miles away, it was easy to conceal my secret during our weekly Sunday night phone conversations. Sam's parents must be forgiving, letting her move back home with a baby.

I felt safe going to their house. They already lived through the unwed mother scandal with their own daughter, so my state would be less of a shock to them. All Catholics knew you didn't break certain rules and didn't discuss certain subjects. Sex was one of the taboo subjects. When I went off to college, innocent and pure, my mom told me not to have sex. If I did, she added, I should go to the health center and get on the pill, but she didn't want to know about it. The proof that her daughter was a sexual being engaging in sex was more than she could handle. So it made perfect sense to delay telling her about my pregnancy.

Why was it so hard for her to accept my carnal nature? Somewhere along the way, I heard the message that sexuality was bad. The seeds of shame had been planted in my soul years ago. Each surrender to the flesh fertilized more seeds until the shame grew so large that it could no longer be contained on the inside. It manifested on the outside for the whole world to see.

My round belly revealed my secret to the whole world. I could not bear the thought of revealing the secret to my parents, shattering their image of me as a pure little girl. The thought of losing their love was worse than the pain of going through this alone.

My face must have revealed my fear. The conductor walked by and stopped at my seat. "Are you okay?" she asked.

"I'm fine," I lied.

"Ticket?"

"Yes." I pulled out the envelope Father Charlie had given me and handed her my train ticket.

The train side rail lights had dimmed creating a lounge-like atmosphere. I fumbled through my bag to find my paperback. I opened it and began reading a new story.

"Rochester!" yelled the conductor over the loud speaker. I prepared to depart, gathering my personal things, putting myself together for my introduction to the family of my priest friend.

Father Charlie assured me that his family was excited to meet me. I struggled to believe my arrival would be met with open arms but did allow myself to hope for the comfort of a home.

The train labored and rocked before coming to a stop. The conductor stepped through the sliding metal door. "Rochester," she said again.

I stood up. The door slid open, and steps magically appeared. With my purse on one shoulder and overnight bag in my hand, I stepped down each stair like an old lady entering a pool, holding tight to the tiled edge.

I gripped the rail with one hand and held my bag with the other. Once both feet landed on the platform, I set down my bag for a short break. Passengers pranced down the stairs behind me, eager to meet their people.

"Aunt Sally!" a young woman squealed as a middle-age woman approached her with open arms. "How was your trip? Have you eaten?" she asked.

I overheard the niece promising her aunt a home-cooked meal of beef stew and biscuits. My mouth began to water. All I could do was stand there and wait, hoping Charlie's father would recognize me. I watched Aunt Sally exit the platform and walk down the stairs. As she disappeared out of view, a tall, lean man appeared at the top of the stairs. I studied him for a second. Black dress slacks, draping over black shiny shoes. A long wool top coat that hung just below his knees. His short hair was coal black with slivers of silver. A beret hid his face, but I could see tortoise-shell glasses. From first glance he looked smart, educated, and wealthy. I looked behind me to scan the crowd to see if he belonged to one of them. But he walked toward me. As he got closer, I could see more detail of his face. It was smooth, clean shaven, and looked a lot like Charlie's.

He lifted his arm to wave. Yep, that was his dad. "Gracie?" he said my name as a question.

"Yes, it's me," I said. He extended his arm and shook my gloved hand.

"I'm Bruce, Charlie's father."

"Nice to meet you." He grabbed my bag, and we walked to the end of the platform and down the stairs.

"I'm over here," he said.

We walked to the parking lot in awkward silence. At least, for me it felt awkward. He led the way in a purposeful manner. His whole demeanor was light and graceful. A true gentleman. He opened the car door, and I climbed in. The interior was warm and soft. He started the engine, and a burst of classical music filled the interior. With a steady hand he spun the dial, and the volume decreased. Eager to break the silence I blurted out, "Nice car." And then felt stupid for stating the obvious. He turned his head slightly to me and smiled.

"Just sit back and relax. You must be tired from the long train ride. We have about a forty-minute drive to the house."

"Okay, thanks."

I stretched out my long legs, leaned back, and rested easily in his care.

Forty-five minutes later I stepped out of the cocoon into the cold, biting winter air.

"Let's get you inside by the fire, where it's warm," he said.

I paused a second, taking in my new environment. The trees were barren but alive. Dry flowerbeds and pine green shrubs framed the front picture window. I felt far away from the concrete city. The house was old but well cared for. It looked like the Waltons' house with its many upstairs windows. I imagined them all snug in bed, calling out to one another in the night, "Good night, Charlie. Good night, Sam."

Father Charlie had shared a little of Sam's story. She was finishing school at the local community college and raising Ben, her eight-month-old son. I wondered if she ever considered terminating her pregnancy as I did. I knew a few girls in college who had abortions. They went to the clinic and had their mistake erased.

Bruce opened the heavy blue door. On the other side was a woman with the short, stout frame of an English teapot. Out of her spout came a high-pitched sound: "You must be Gracie! Please, come in and get warm."

In one quick movement she bolted the door, removed my coat, and spun around to kiss Charlie's father.

"Tea?" she asked.

"Yes," I said.

Bruce watched his wife scurry about with pure delight. With his eyes set on her flushed cheeks, he said, "This is my wife, Beth, the better half."

"So nice to meet you," I said in my best mannered voice. I sat down on the sofa by the fire and warmed my toes.

"I hope you two are hungry. I've got a roast in the oven and warm rolls for our supper," she said.

They acted as if everything was normal. No mention of the elephant in my belly. I relaxed into the country and enjoyed a hot meal, eating one too many biscuits smothered in butter. Later I snuggled into my twin bed and pulled the warm cotton quilt up to my nose. I buried my face in the down pillow and inhaled the fresh air. I allowed my heavy body to let go. For the first time in a long time I felt loved.

I hugged my baby belly. "Is this how you feel, baby? All nestled inside the warm womb?" I smiled. "I promise to keep you safe, my sweet baby." I felt a little kick.

CHAPTER 19

The sun's rays filtered in through the cotton curtains and invited me to begin a new day. I stretched long and deep and lifted my body out of its quilted cradle. Walking toward the window, I caught my reflection in the silver-framed mirror that hung over the antique dresser. I almost didn't recognize myself. My skin looked smoother and moist. My eyes were soft and rested. It indeed had been beauty sleep. With a tug of the window shade the room was illuminated with a splash of sun. I stood and soaked in the heat. Closing my eyes, I was transported back to the beach. The memory of sun, sand, and ocean breezes surfaced to my consciousness.

A memory popped up like a jack-in-the-box. I must have been six or seven years old. I sat in the sand building castles at the sea's edge. Bright orange buckets surrounded me, and I had a green shovel in my hand. Not spilling a grain, I scooped the sand in the bigger pail, patting it down between scoops, just like my mom taught me. I filled it to the brim and patted it down, like a cup of brown sugar. Grabbing the pail with both hands, I flipped it like a fried egg. With both hands I lifted the bucket with the skill of surgeon, careful not to collapse my tower of sand. Pleased by my creation, I would begin again, this time scooping into the slightly smaller pail. I set it perfectly centered on top of the first. One by one, I would add a smaller mound to the top until my tower was as tall as me.

The next step was a search of the shore for sticks and shells, the necessary materials to build a moat and bridge. With the biggest stick I could carry, I traced a circle in the sand around my creation to define the moat. I scooped the circle deep with my toy shovel and then patted the walls tight. I strategically placed shells in the wall for support and flare. Once the wall was strong, I ran to the sea to fill my bucket with the salty water so I could fill up my freshly created moat.

Running up to higher ground, the safe spot for my castle, I would pour the sea water into my well. One more trip and it would be filled. On to the bridge. I formed it out of my dry sticks and twigs. It was perfect.

Stepping back, I admired my work and smiled with a sense of accomplishment. My best castle ever. Eager to share my master creation, I sprinted up the log steps to our summer cabin. I was so excited. "Daddy!" I screamed. "Daddy, come quick! I have something to show you."

He was sitting on the screened porch reading his paper. He peeked out from behind the page. "New castle?"

"Yes! But it's really big this time. It even has a moat with a bridge just like you taught me to build! Come down now, Daddy," I pleaded.

Without wasting a second, he put down his paper and grabbed my hand and let me lead his six-foot-six frame down the log steps.

"It's right down there, Daddy," I said, so excited for him to see.

"Okay, babe, I am coming."

Once my feet hit the sand, I broke free of his hand and ran to the spot in the sand where I left my creation. Dad jogged behind me with a look of anticipation on his face. But when I reached the beach I couldn't find it. I ran back and forth, like a lost puppy. Where did it go?

My castle had been drowned by the sea. All that remained were three tiny sticks from the little drawbridge.

"Daddy!" I cried. "It's gone! I built the best one, and the ocean took it away!" I spotted a broken shell and ran to fetch it. Another stick sat by my yellow pail. "I wanted you to see it so much." I choked out the words through tears "I'm sorry, Daddy," I cried. "I wanted you to see it."

He knelt down beside me and pulled me into his arms. "It's okay, honey. The tide came in early. We can build a new one together," he said. "We will build up here on higher ground so the waves can't get it."

"Okay, Daddy."

In silence I gathered my shovel and three little pails. I brought them up to my father, sitting on higher ground. He knelt beside me, knees deep in the sand. Together we scooped, and we patted. Soon our castle grew taller and stronger. When it passed my height, Dad lifted me up and let me build it taller. It was bigger and stronger than me. And this time it survived the tide.

CHAPTER 20

"Gracie," a voice whispered through the closed door. "You awake yet?" asked Beth.

"Yes, come in. Just making the bed," I said, smoothing down the yellow quilt.

Beth entered. "Good morning, dear. Did you sleep well?"

"Oh, yes, the best sleep I've had in months."

"Oh, good to hear. I have some waffles for you downstairs. Ready for breakfast?"

"Yes." I could hardly wait for breakfast. The smell of fresh brewed coffee and cinnamon floated up the stairs.

"Great. Samantha and Ben are downstairs and are eager to meet you," she said.

My eyes opened wider. I almost forgot I was meeting them today. "Be right down."

Ben was a husky baby boy. He had thick, sturdy little legs and chubby arms. He crawled on the kitchen floor in his corduroy overalls. He looked like the Gerber baby. He scooted around the corner and plopped on his bottom. He had found a crumb he was examining in his fat fingers. He must have felt me staring at him from the bottom of the stairs. He looked up, studied my face, and then broke into a toothless grin.

"What are you giggling about?" said someone in a soft voice.

Two seconds later Samantha appeared. She looked at her son and then up at me. She scooped up her boy and walked toward me. "Hi, I'm Samantha—Sam, actually," she said. "And this little guy is Ben. He is so excited to meet you."

"Hi, Ben." I reached out to shake his little hand. But he pulled his hand back and tucked his curly-haired head into his mom's breast.

"Oh, now you're going to play shy," she said.

"So glad to finally meet you, Sam," I said. "Charlie has told me so much about you."

"I hope only the good stuff."

"Of course."

"Have a seat," she said. "Mom kept the waffles hot for you."

"They smell delicious. I'm starving."

"I remember those days. I was always hungry when I was carrying this little guy," she said. "And he still eats everything in sight!"

Ben squirmed to get out of her arms and back to the floor for more exploring. Sam bent down to release him, and he crawled right out of her arms. She sat with me as I ate my waffles and bacon.

"Orange juice?"

"Sure."

As she poured my juice she asked, "So how long have you been attending Charlie's church?"

"Umm," I hesitated. I'd gone only a few times. I wasn't a faithful Catholic church-goer. "Not that long. I just met him a couple months ago."

Sam set the pitcher of juice down. "I'm glad you met him. He's a good brother."

"Yes, he must be. He's been helping me a lot."

"Yeah, he helped me a lot last year when I was going through all of this. It was a scary time."

I nodded and sipped my juice. Sam seemed so confident and sure of herself. It was hard to imagine her being afraid. She carried herself with the grace of a ballerina. So neat and petite. Her complexion was clear, and her long hair hung loosely around her shoulders, the color matching Ben's. "Charlie is a good listener. I'd talk to him for hours on the phone, and he let me go on and on." Sam lifted a hot mug of coffee to her lips. She hugged the cup with both hands and savored the sip. "I don't know how I would have made it without him."

Beth popped her head into the kitchen. "Hi, girls. You getting acquainted? Where's the baby?" Ben was sitting on the floor in the corner of the kitchen playing with a Cheerio he had found. Beth spotted him. "Icky! Give me that, sweetie. You don't want to eat that." She grimaced.

But Ben disagreed. He didn't mind a little dust on his cereal. As Beth reached down to snatch it from his hand, he screamed in opposition.

"Come here. I will get you more." Beth lifted him from the cold floor and plunked him in his dinosaur-covered high chair. She poured out a cup of cereal onto his tray for him to eat.

Sam looked over. "Mom, what are you doing?" she scolded. "He's already had his breakfast."

"I know," she said. "I just gave him a few to keep him happy."

"All that kid does is eat," said Sam, smiling at her happy, chubby boy.

"Oh, Sam, you're so dramatic. He's perfectly healthy. He eats more now because he's crawling around everywhere."

Ben slammed his tiny hand on his tray, and Cheerios flew everywhere. He laughed like it was a game.

"Oh, so that's how you do it, getting them on the floor. I'm watching you, buddy," cooed Beth.

I finished my breakfast and brought my dishes into the kitchen.

"Just set them in the sink, dear. I will get them," said Beth. "After I put this little mess maker down for his morning nap."

"Oh, Mom, you don't have to do it. I've got him," said Sam.

"No, no. You have a guest. Let me take the baby, and you and Gracie spend some time together."

"All right, thanks, Mom," said Sam. She walked over to her mom and gave her a hug and then leaned down, picking up all the scattered Cheerios. She leaned over Ben's high chair. "You're gonna spend the afternoon with Grandma. Be good, little guy," she said. Then she kissed his soft cheek and messed up his curly hair. Looking back at me, she asked, "What would you like to do today?"

"I'm not sure," I answered.

"You could go into town," Beth suggested. "It's not too cold today, and the sun is shining."

"That's an idea," said Sam. "Or we could go for a walk down by the lake. It's frozen, but so beautiful this time of year. What sounds good to you, Grace?"

"Either one is fine with me," I answered.

"Okay then. You up for a walk? It's not too far. About a half mile down the trail."

I felt as if Sam wanted to go to the lake. My people-pleasing personality went along with the suggestion, even though I really did not want to take a hike.

"As long as you don't walk too fast, I'll go."

"Perfect! I'll bring some hot chocolate, and we will head down in about twenty minutes," she said. "Does that give you enough time to get ready?"

"Sure." I didn't bring boots or hiking shoes. I'd be hiking in my tennis shoes.

Beth scrubbed Ben's face with a washcloth, and he protested with screaming. "Be careful, you two," she said. "Don't walk out on the lake too far."

"Oh, Mom, you worry too much," said Sam.

"No. I just know my daughter," said Beth.

Beth kissed Sam on the head and carried Ben upstairs, singing, "This old man, he played one. . . ."

Sam got me some mittens and a hat from the downstairs closet. "Here, you can use these. They're warm."

"Thanks," I said. And we both walked upstairs to get ready for our adventure.

CHAPTER 21

The crunch of dry leaves hidden under snow was the only sound I could hear as Sam and I trekked single-file down the trail that led to the frozen lake. Cold, clean air slapped my cheeks as I walked, but I didn't mind as much as I thought I would. My insides felt warm, and my energy was renewed in this country air.

"It's only about another quarter mile. You doing okay?" called Sam. She stopped to look back at me trudging through the shallow snow. Her pace was faster than mine, but I was keeping up. It felt good to have a little space between us. Time to gather my thoughts and rehearse what I wanted to ask her.

"I'm good," I said. "Just a little slower these days."

She nodded and kept going toward the lake. I wondered if she had had doubts about keeping little Ben. If she did, you sure couldn't tell now. She was such a good mother. It looked so easy and natural watching her with Ben. I wondered if I could do it. I always wanted to be a mom. I remember playing Barbies as a young girl with my neighbor friends. We built elaborate houses out of blocks and plastic, pink furniture for our pretend families. We all had various versions of Ken as our husband, along with two adorable, blonde baby girls. They didn't make baby Barbie boys.

For hours we played, living in the world of make-believe. I knew that's how it would be for me. I'd grow up, go to college, and then meet my perfect "Ken." We would have the most romantic courtship followed by a big beautiful garden wedding. Then honeymoon in Hawaii, come home and build our dream house. I would have four children: two girls and two boys. Of course I would be a stay-at-home mom, drive carpool, and bake brownies. It would be the perfect life, just like my plastic, Barbie world.

I realized I was living in a fantasy world. Dreams don't always come true. Men don't always love you. And babies come when you don't plan on them.

Lost in my thoughts, I wasn't paying attention to the trail and tripped over a fallen log. Down on my knees I went, bracing my fall with my mittened hands.

Sam heard the snap of the branch and looked back to see me on all fours. "Gracie!" she yelled. "You okay?" She ran back the thirty feet to check the damage. I felt frozen in the snow.

"Here, grab my hand," she said. She helped me up and held on to me until I found my balance.

"Thanks," I said. "I don't know what happened. I was walking and then *bam*, I was on the ground."

"Yeah, a lot of branches and tree limbs are hiding under the snow. I should have warned you about them. Just go slow," she said.

"Yeah, a warning would have been helpful." I was angry. Not so much at her, but at myself. I was beginning to think we should have gone into town. I shook the snow off my mittens and took a deep breath. Sam waited and slowed her pace, walking only a few steps ahead of me.

"When I was pregnant with Ben, I was so clumsy. Always banging into things."

I wondered if she was lying just to make me feel better. Because she did not look like the type to bang into things. Her slender, dancer body moved with grace, even now, trudging through the snow-packed trail.

"Yeah, I'm not too graceful right now," I joked.

"Hang in there," she said. "Just a few more months and you will have your body back."

"How long did it take you?" I asked. "To get your figure back?"

"Since I nursed Ben, it only took about eight weeks. Nursing is the way to go. Burns a lot of calories," she said. She did a quick back-pedal. "I mean, if you are planning to keep the baby."

The next ten minutes we walked in silence.

I had no answers for her. All I could think of were questions. A million questions.

"Did you know, right away, that you were going to keep him?" I asked.

"No. I was confused," she said. "When Brent told me he was not ready to be a dad and was staying at school, I didn't know what to do. I thought he'd be there, but he wasn't. That's when I called Charlie. He helped me sort it all out," she said. "I mean, I knew, like you, that I wanted to be a mother, but not like this. It didn't fit my plan."

"Did you consider giving him up?" I asked.

"I did. I thought about it. Even met with a counselor at an adoption agency. But after seeking God and spending a lot of time in prayer with Charlie, I knew I was supposed to keep him and raise him in the Lord," she said. "For me, that was the best choice. But it is different for every girl."

"What about your parents?" I asked. "What did they want you to do?"

"They were supportive either way," she said. "They said they would help me, but they weren't going to raise him for me. I had to take full responsibility, so it was my choice."

"Wow, they sound like amazing parents," I said. "I'm not sure my parents will handle it that well."

"You mean you haven't told them?" She sounded a little shocked.

"No. I've been too afraid. But I will soon."

"Why don't you call them while you are here with us? Then you won't have to do it alone."

That sounded like a good idea to me. Her mom was so calm. Maybe she could talk to my mom. My mom would not be calm.

"Maybe," I said.

"We will do it together. You have to tell them, Gracie. It's their grandchild."

I didn't think of it like that, but she was right.

"Your parents are so calm," I said. "It must have been easy for you."

"Oh, don't let them fool you. We all cried our share of tears. It wasn't easy in the beginning, but somehow God brought us all through it together." She hesitated. "Have you talked to God about it?"

"You mean, prayed?"

"No. I mean, have a heart-to-heart conversation with God," she said. "Did you ask God what you should do?"

"Ask God?"

"Yeah. That's what I did. I asked Him, and He directed my steps. He told me what to do and gave me the strength to do it."

"He told you? Like audibly spoke to you?"

"Not audibly, like a scene from *The Ten Commandments*, but He spoke in a still, small voice deep in my spirit. It was peaceful. I just knew that I knew."

I could not answer that. I stared at her in awe and with a little envy. I wish I heard that same voice and God would tell me what to do.

"There it is!" Sam pointed at the lake. "Isn't it gorgeous?"

It was spectacular. Much bigger than I imagined.

"There's a bench down this bend. Let's go take a break and sit. It's right on the edge," she said.

Taking deliberate steps, I walked off the trail and down the incline heading to the bench. Sam brushed off the snow with her mittens so we could sit.

"Have a seat," she said with a big smile. I was so happy to sit down. We sat together gazing out over the frozen lake. It looked like a sheet of glass, cold and pristine.

We stared in silence for a while. Content in the solace of the frozen white world. And then I dared to break the silence.

"So tell me again, how do you hear from God?"

"Just listen. Quiet. He's here, with us now."

I looked at Sam. Her eyes were shut. I didn't know what to do, so I shut my eyes too. And waited. Waited to hear. To listen. To hear God speak. But all I heard was quiet. Maybe the wind in the trees, but no voice. I squeezed my eyes together tighter, straining to hear God speak. But nothing. And then a voice started speaking in my own head. *You are so stupid! Why would God want to talk to you? You're pregnant, not married, and a horrible girl. You failed him. Your sins are too many to count. You have a lot of good deeds to do to make up for what you screwed up. You will never catch up. Why even try? It is pointless. The other guys you slept with, the lies you told. You can never make this okay with God. It's unforgiveable. You knew sex outside of marriage was wrong. But you did it anyway. Now God is punishing you. He doesn't love you. He won't speak to you. You are not worthy. You are worthless. Dirty as filthy rags.*

I tried to push the critical voice out of my head. But it kept getting louder, accusing me of terrible things. I knew that what it was saying was true, so how could I fight it?

For the first time in my life I felt remorse over the choices I had made. How I wished for a second chance. A do-over. But so much had happened. How could I erase it all and start over fresh? It was hopeless. Tears streamed down my face. A dark, ugly pit burned in my belly. I felt a stabbing pain in my center and sensed it wanted to suck me into its hole. I could not control its power. It rose higher and higher and lodged in my throat. It possessed an energy that could not be stopped. I could not hold it in any longer. My mouth opened, and the sound that came out scared both me and Sam out of the serene, silent moment. I bent over, heaving in pain. Groans and moans came forth from deep in my belly. I didn't even recognize the sounds as me. Something deep inside was being pulled out by the roots by some invisible force.

Sam stayed calm and started praying in a soft voice using words I never heard. The moans came like vomit. Finally, nothing was left. And then came the flood of tears. Streams of water ran down my face and landed in the snow, melting the cold ice. Sam put her hand on my back and rubbed it. "Is there more?" she asked. "Just let it out. All of it."

I held the sides of the bench preparing for more. I thought I was done. But then there was one long, deep moan. And then it was over.

I felt empty but calm. The tears flowed freely, but the force had left. These tears felt different from tears of fear. They were more like tears of cleansing, sweet and peaceful. They soothed my soul, and I didn't hold them back.

Sam held me as tears bounced off my parka. Somehow she knew what was going on, even if I didn't. I took comfort in her knowing.

"You feel better now?" Sam asked.

My face relaxed into a smile, and laughter burst from my belly. I could not stop smiling or laughing. "What just happened to me?" I asked her.

"You just got rid of some junk you didn't need. Some old hidden pain from the past. God delivered you from the lies of the enemy. He is working in you, you know. He chips away at all the ugly, dark stuff until something beautiful emerges. He goes slow, layer by layer. It can hurt, but when you surrender and go with it you will finally be free," she said. "With each chunk that He frees, more of the precious stone is revealed. That's your true self. That's how God sees you."

I was captivated by every word. Even though I did not fully comprehend it, I knew Sam spoke truth.

I felt different. Lighter, cleaner. The sun started to go down, close to the surface of the lake. Sam and I gazed a few more minutes, savoring the glow. A beam of sunlight penetrated a spot on the lake right where my eyes were focused. Its brilliance made me feel brand-new, like a new creation—and maybe even a little beautiful.

CHAPTER 22

The fire crackled and popped. Sparks flew out, but dissipated in the cool air. I sat as close as possible to the open flame soaking up every ounce of heat. Bruce came into the living room with a mug in his hand. "Warm enough?" he asked. He grinned at me through his straight teeth.

"Yes, I'm getting there," I answered.

"This should help," he said as he handed me the mug of hot chocolate. "You and Sam had some walk today. You'll sleep well tonight."

"Yes, I hope so," I said. My mind was not in the present moment, knowing I had to make the call to my parents in just a few minutes. Beth and Bruce offered to talk to my parents with me, and I was glad for the backup. I couldn't believe I had waited so long. But each time I picked up the phone to tell them I couldn't do it. Fear and shame kept me in denial. What they didn't know couldn't hurt them. Isn't that what my mom meant by telling me to go to the health center and get the pill but don't tell her about it?

She didn't want to know. She couldn't handle the truth. It made me wonder what things had happened to her that she couldn't tell me about. There were things hidden. Like a beautifully painted Easter egg, she was bright and cheerful on the outside. But if the shell broke it would be an ugly mess. My mom never let her shell break. She appeared perfect. She required her children to be perfect as well. So I pretended to be perfect, even if it meant telling a lie. But eventually everything that is hidden comes out in the light.

Beth handed me the cold receiver. I dialed the number from memory. Dad answered on the fourth ring. "Hi, Dad, it's Grace."

"Hi, Grace, how are things?"

"Good, good." I was on autopilot. "Just visiting some friends in the country for the weekend."

"Oh, that's nice. Getting out of the city."

"Yeah, it's a nice break."

"I'll go get your mom."

"Okay. Dad, wait. When you get Mom, I need you to stay on the other line. I need to talk to you both," I said with a quiver in my voice.

"Okay," he said, a bit less cheerful. "I'll go get your mother."

Usually Dad would ask me about my job, and then we'd talk about the weather, and then he would give the phone to Mom. She and I would talk awhile, sometimes a whole hour. She would update me on the lives of my siblings, reciting a list of their accomplishments.

Her perky voice picked up the phone. "Hi, Grace!"

"Hi, Mom. How are you?"

"I'm good. How are you? Dad said you wanted to talk to us both?"

I gulped. "Yes. I need to tell you something."

There was a long pause.

"Remember the guy I met who lives on the beach?"

"No, not sure you told us about him," she said.

"Well, I met him and have been going out there on the weekends. I mean, I was, in the summer."

They didn't acknowledge what I just said. So I kept going.

"Well, it happened only once. But. . .I'm so sorry to tell you this. . .I'm pregnant."

The words physically hurt as I said them. My face felt painful. I couldn't breathe. The response was immediate. My mom let out a loud gasp and started crying uncontrollably. I couldn't hear my dad. He said something to my mom and then asked me, "How far along are you?"

"About six months," I answered.

My mom's cries got louder, and I couldn't handle her pain and disappointment.

"Dad, the people where I'm staying want to talk to you. Here's Beth. I'm so sorry, Dad." And I handed the phone to Beth. I couldn't listen. I ran into the kitchen and cried. Sam was there, ready to comfort me.

"My parents will talk to them. It will be okay," she said.

Bruce and Beth talked to my parents for what felt like a long hour. I waited in the kitchen, sipping my hot chocolate. When the conversation ended, they both came in to join me and Sam. We all sat in silence at the kitchen table. Bruce spoke first.

"I know that wasn't easy, but you did the right thing," he said. "Your dad will calm your mom down. It will be okay. Just give them some time to process this news."

Time. We were running out of time. The baby was coming in a few months. I wasn't so sure time would heal this wound.

After Patrick and I broke up, my mom pleaded with me to come home. But my pride wouldn't allow it. Even though my relationship with Patrick failed, I wanted to prove to myself and my parents that I didn't fail. I was determined to make it in New York. So I stayed. With each passing day I lost myself a little more.

My identity had been so tied up in Patrick and in his love that I did not feel whole. I desperately searched to fill the love void with meaningless acts of lust. I searched for external encounters to fill something deeply internal.

My dad told Bruce to tell me to call him when I got back into the city. I said okay. But in my heart I wanted to run away.

Beth shared with me how she felt when she first found out Sam was pregnant. "It was devastating because I loved her so much," she said. "Your mom feels the same way about you. But she will come around. Just be patient." I wanted to believe Beth but wasn't too sure. At least now they knew. The secret was exposed.

"Tomorrow's a new day," said Bruce. "It's time to retire." He patted my shoulder and then climbed up the wooden staircase. "You coming, my love?" he called down to Beth.

"Yes, dear. Be right up," she said. She looked at me with sadness and compassion. "Try to get some sleep tonight, my dear. Give it over to God."

Sam and I sat in silence and finished our hot chocolate.

"The hardest part is over," she said.

"Is it?" I asked.

CHAPTER 23

Sam is a good mom, I thought as I boarded the train home to the Bronx. She made it look so easy, but Ben was a cutie pie and seemed like an easy baby. I wondered if I would have an easy baby. I looked down at my belly. "Will you be easy? What kind of baby are you?" For the first time in months I felt excited—this great anticipation. I was excited to meet this little person who had been growing inside me for the past six months. Would she look like me? Or Lee? And once I met him or her, could I give him up to another mom?

I knew it was selfish to keep my baby for my sake. I had to think of what was best for the baby. She came first. What would she want?

Even though I didn't continue Lamaze classes with Glenda, I met regularly with my midwife, Kim. She had an office in the West Village. It looked more like an art gallery than a medical office. Kim partnered with an adoption agency and gave me options in case I chose not to parent my baby. I had sifted through the books that were given to me. They were filled with hopeful and desperate parents, ready to adopt my baby. The photos looked fake. No one could be that happy. I read the bios of couples wanting to adopt children, critiquing each one like a private eye. I peered deep into their eyes, eager to uncover what lay below the surface. I was picky.

Too picky. Only two couples would I even consider meeting. But I kept cancelling my appointments, feeling protective of my little one.

I hoped Lee would come around. We could do this together. We both had jobs with decent paychecks. We could find a little apartment on the island. Lee would find more construction work, and I would wheel our little one down the boardwalk to watch the waves each morning and feed the pigeons.

I saw the women in the Bronx every day pushing babies up and down the street, some two at a time in double strollers. I could do that. I thought of Sam living with her parents. It worked for her. She wasn't alone raising Ben. I had asked her how she knew she was going to keep him. She said, "One morning I woke up, and everything was clear. The veil of confusion had vanished, and I knew without a doubt that God chose me to parent Ben. I just knew, deep inside that hidden place in your soul."

I was so full of doubts. I started praying again. And I prayed the doubts would go away.

CHAPTER 24

"Taxi! Taxi!" I yelled. I could not find a cab. I looked up and down Madison Avenue. Normally Madison was crawling with a fleet of yellow cabs picking up and dropping off high-paid executives. I blinked my eyes a few times. My vision seemed blurry this morning. Was it my eyes? Or was the smog bad today? It was like a thin veil covering my pupils. I blinked again, forcing the tears to cleanse my eyes.

The last couple months had flown by. I still was working and doing a lot of soul searching. I took an early lunch to fit in my midwife appointment. It was at 11:15. I dreaded being late. Kim was always overbooked, and I knew I would have to wait as it was. Usually I would walk or take the train, but my bulging belly, coupled with my swollen ankles, begged me to take a taxi.

I stopped walking and stood on the corner of 47th and Madison. Sooner or later an available cab would have to come by. I closed my eyes as I stood on the corner and let the world move around me. I felt invisible. I could hear the street sounds, cars honking, vendor carts rolling, people scurrying up and down the avenue.

Suddenly I felt a beam of light penetrate through the haze that hovered over the city. The beam broke through the clouds and landed on my chest. The heat penetrated my blouse and touched my skin like a warm blanket. Spring felt so good—a teaser of what was to come and a reminder of the cold dark winter just behind me.

As the heat soothed my skin, the tears finally came, dissolving the veil clouding my vision. A blast of a horn jolted me out of my internal world. Two feet in front of me a yellow cab swerved to park. A young executive stepped out right in front of me. He almost backed into my belly.

"Excuse me," he said. "You look like you need this." He held open the back door.

Surprised by my good fortune, I said, "Yes," and climbed in the back seat.

My lucky cab looked brand-new. Straight off the assembly line. Not even a crack in the black seats. My driver had a clean, friendly face. I doubted he was a New Yorker, and when he opened his mouth to speak I found out I was correct.

Fresh off the boat from Dublin, his name was Paul. And he spoke in a thick Irish brogue.

"Top of the day to ya, lassie." He winked at me through the rear-view mirror. "Where may I take you?"

"Downtown," I said, "Nineteenth and Seventh Avenue."

"Right away, lass. Your chariot awaits," he joked.

Paul kept sneaking peeks at me through the rear-view mirror. He had the grin of a four-year-old boy in trouble. I unbuttoned my top button, enjoying the pleasant heat.

"Spring is here," he said.

"I know. I've been waiting."

"And it looks like spring might be bringing you a wee gift."

"Yes." I smiled.

A spirit of joy engulfed the cab. It radiated off my young driver. He almost bounced in his seat as he swerved in and out of midtown traffic. Paul tapped the button on his radio. He played the music a little loud and hummed to the melody. It was a familiar song, but I had not heard it in a long time.

"I can see clearly now, the rain has gone. . .birds in the sky. It's gonna be a bright, bright, sunshiny day."

How appropriate, I thought. The music put me in a happy mood. One song ended, and another happy song would begin. "Here Comes the Sun" by the Beatles played next. I noticed a little theme to his music.

"What station are you playing?" I asked the driver.

"Oh, my sweet, it's not a station. It's a mixed tape I made myself. Just felt the urge to play it for you," he said. "You looked a little bushed when you first got in."

"Do you do this for all your fares?"

"Nah, only when the Spirit leads," he said.

"Spirit?"

"Spirit of God," he said. "You got to listen to it when it calls."

Another person who hears from God. This was strange. Maybe it was possible to hear God's voice.

"You a believer?" he asked.

"I guess," I said with a little doubt.

"Don't guess. Have faith. It's a choice."

"I'm Catholic," I said.

"Catholic is a religion. What I'm talking about is a relationship with God. . .no religion can teach you that. It's supernatural."

I remembered the incident at the frozen lake. And the talks with Sam. I felt as if something bigger than me was coming closer, coming near. Maybe this was God.

"Don't think about it too much," he said. "You're a thinker… I can tell. Just receive it. God loves you, ya know. And He has a plan for your life."

His words rang true, and I felt this peace in the center of my being.

We slowed to a stop on Fifth Avenue. Traffic was barely moving.

The driver turned and looked back at me. "Just like you are about to give birth to that precious little baby, you can be born again in Jesus. You can start fresh."

"Okay, now you are making me cry. I was so joyful, and now tears. Why?"

"Just let the tears flow. The Spirit is touching you. Let Him have His way," he said.

"I know," I said. "But you don't know all I have done. Can God forgive that?"

"Yes, God forgives everything. He knows all the bad stuff about you anyway and still loves you. He sees you through the blood of His Son, Jesus."

I cried even more. No one ever explained it to me like this. For the first time in a long time I felt hopeful.

"Hold on," he said as he pulled a pair of sunglasses out of the glove compartment. He slid them on his face. "Look here. Imagine that these glasses are as red as this stop light. Blood red. God puts them on before He looks at you. So when He sees you He is looking at you through a filter of His Son's blood. All your sins, failures, flaws are covered, by His Son's blood. It's like they never happened. All is forgiven. You are holy and pure, a new creation in Christ."

My mind struggled to grasp this, and then, like a camera flash, it clicked. The light came on. My eyes were opened.

"So what do I have to do to get this second chance?" I asked.

"Nothing," he said. "It is a free gift. There is nothing you can do. Jesus did it all. You must turn from your old ways, look to Him and just believe and receive it. It's a choice."

Suddenly all the prayers I had said in church on auto pilot made more sense to me. Everything came alive. My sins were washed away. I felt different. For the first time in a long time I felt worthy.

"Okay, we made it. Sorry about the mess on Fifth. You never know what the traffic will be this time of day."

I didn't want to get out of the cab. The peace I felt inside was amazing. I reached in my pocket to get the money to pay my fare.

"Just give me five dollars," he said.

"Really?"

"Yeah, it's the new believers' discount." He winked.

CHAPTER 25

could feel the perspiration inside my pants as I sat on the edge of the exam table waiting for Kim. She was running late, but I didn't care. I was still so elated from my encounter with the cab driver that I felt no anxiety. I closed my eyes and tuned into my innermost being. I could almost hear the baby swooshing around in the water. I knew, deep inside. I knew. She belonged to me. I was her mother, and she was my child.

My doubts went far away. I don't know where they went, but I didn't care. They were gone. I felt strong for the first time in a long time.

Kim gently knocked on the door and then entered the room.

"Hello, Miss Grace? How is Mommy today?"

"I feel good today."

"You look good. Did you cut your hair?"

Running my fingers through my long waves, I answered, "No."

"Hmm. Well, you look really good. Different. So let's take a look at the baby."

I lay flat on my back. Kim massaged the jelly into my belly and then searched for the baby with the scope.

"There it is," she said. "Take a look?"

I turned my head to look at the screen. I could see little arms and legs. The baby looked like an angel floating in water. Tears of joy filled my eyes. That was my baby. And I knew that I knew. I was keeping her. I was her mother.

Kim's smile turned into a look of concern. She crinkled her brow and looked closer at the screen.

"What's wrong?" I asked.

She didn't answer right away and kept looking at the monitor. "Scoot on down."

I scooted.

"I need to take a look at your cervix," she said. "This may be a little cold."

She inserted the metal speculum. I lay still like a statue while she did her exam.

"When did you start spotting?" she asked.

"Spotting? What do you mean? I feel fine."

"Well, I see a little blood. We just need to keep a close eye on it," she said. "If you experience heavy bleeding or any discharge, you need to call me immediately. And for the next few weeks I want you to rest. No work, okay?"

"Okay," I said, like an obedient child. I had to work. Needed to work. I only had one more month before the baby came and needed the income as long as possible. "Is the baby okay?"

"Yes, the baby is fine, but I need you to rest. You don't want to break your water prematurely. I'll give you a note for work," she said. "And then I want to see you back here in three weeks. Set it up with Fran on your way out."

"Okay," I said, a little worried.

"Try not to worry," she said. "You will be all right. We need to be a little cautious here. Call me if you see any more blood."

Blood. All I could think about for the next few days was blood. I went to church that Sunday, and they sang a song called "Nothing but the Blood of Jesus." Everything was about blood. I kept an eye on my own body, looking for any blood. I stayed home from work and rested. Wendy wasn't too happy about it, but she couldn't do anything. I thought I'd go crazy lying in bed but it was turning out to be a nice break. I divided my time between the hard futon and soft couch. I stayed in the apartment and read books, watched movies, and ate anything I craved. Jason stopped by midweek and brought me a gallon of jamocha almond fudge. I was so happy I kissed his cheek.

Sheila periodically checked on me and brought me tea and cookies. When she could break free from her babies she'd sneak downstairs, and we would chat for hours. It was usually late in the night by the time Bryan got home from the train and her little ones were all tucked snugly into their beds.

I told her about the blood. And the song at church about the blood. She knew it.

"We sang that song back in Sunday school years ago," she mused.

Sheila's mother was Catholic, but her dad was a Presbyterian. An old Irish feud could not quench their love. So Sheila grew up attending both Presbyterian Sunday school and Catholic mass. "When you get down to it," she said, "both faiths are quite similar. Both believe Jesus died for our sins. His shed blood was for us—to save us from eternal separation from God.

"Without the shedding of the blood, the sacrifice for our sins, there could be no atonement. The blood is the most important thing. It's the blood of Jesus that saves. Nothing more, and nothing less," she said.

It was so simple. I wondered why I could not see it before.

The apartment door buzzer was going off like crazy. Buzz, buzz, buzz.

"Coming!" I yelled. It took me a few minutes to roll to my side and push myself up to sitting. Then I had to stand. I had gained over forty pounds, and it was all in front. I made it to the door after the nineteenth buzz.

"Who is it?" I called as I moved the metal pole and unlocked the dead bolt.

"It's me, Sheila," she called back. "Bryan's home with the wee ones. He's working a split shift today. I only have about twenty minutes." She came in carrying a brown cardboard box. She set it on the floor and wrapped her skinny arms around my round body. "I'm so happy for you! You're keeping the baby!" she exclaimed. "Bryan told me after he saw you on the train. He said you looked so happy. What made you make your decision?"

"After my trip to the country I started praying, or more like talking to God. I asked Him every day if He wanted me to keep this one."

"And He said yes?"

"Not at first. He was quiet. I couldn't hear anything. And over time things kept happening."

"What kind of things?" she asked.

"You know, like coincidences, but they weren't coincidences. It felt more orchestrated. It's hard to explain."

"I know what you mean. My grandmother used to always say, 'There are no coincidences with God. He has a plan.'"

"Yes! That is exactly how it felt. Like He was planning all these events. It was like there was a breeze leading me, guiding me along a path, directing my steps. Before I knew it, I was where He wanted me to be. I don't know how I got there, but it felt true. I didn't feel so alone. Then one day I just knew. Just like Sam said I would. I knew God wanted me to be a mother to this child. And I said yes."

Sheila squealed in excitement and hugged me again. "You'll be the best mommy!"

"I'm gonna try," I said. "I know I've made some bad choices, but I think now I have the power to make good ones. And I believe God forgives me."

"Oh, child, of course He forgives you. You are His precious daughter, and He loves you so much. That's why He can take our bad choices and, if we turn back to Him and trust Him, He turns them into a beautiful gift. God knows what we will choose before we choose it. But He is a gentleman. He lets us do it our way, and when it doesn't work out He cleans up our mess."

"That's some crazy kind of love," I said.

"Yes, it is God's love. You'll know it when you first lay eyes on this baby. It's unconditional."

"I feel so overwhelmed by love," I told her. "Why did it take me so long to find it?"

"We block it. Sometimes with shame. Sometimes with guilt, anger, you name it. But when we let go, watch out! God comes pouring in with His love. He brings beauty out of ashes, order from chaos, and life out of death. His love covers it all."

Sheila pulled out a little yellow dress from the cardboard box. "Look at this!" she exclaimed. She pressed the dress with her hand and laid it on the table. Next, she pulled out a tiny pair of denim pants and a blue and white striped shirt to match. "Oh, I remember when Scott wore these. He was so adorable. Now he's so big. They grow up so fast."

As Sheila was oohing and ahhing over baby clothes, my mind raced ahead. I needed so much other stuff for the baby. A crib, changing table, swing—the list went on. Sheila saw my panicked face.

"Relax, Gracie. You will have everything you need. No worries. Now sit down and look at this wee little sundress. It has a matching bonnet."

CHAPTER 26

*N*esting. That's what they call it when an expectant mother frantically gathers supplies and cleans every corner of her home. I was scrubbing the bassinet Sheila gave me with bleach and a toothbrush at two in the morning. I washed baby sheets, baby blankets, and baby clothes, all in a special detergent designed especially for babies. I found a white wicker changing table, just like the one my mom used with all four of us. It was on clearance in a discount store in the Bronx. I bought it with my last paycheck from work. My due date was fast approaching, and I wanted to be ready.

At night I would lie in bed and make mental lists. Labor bag, clock to time contractions, soothing music tape for labor. Breathing instructions. Warm socks for labor. Outfit to take baby home in. . .and on and on my mind went. It was difficult to fall asleep most nights. I glanced at the green neon numbers on my clock—11:11. Sleep was not coming. I shifted my position to my side placing a pillow between my legs. Then I got hungry. I wanted ice cream.

Linda, one of the women in my new birthing group at the hospital, told a story of how her husband got up at three in the morning, walked down to the bodega, and bought her a gallon of strawberry ice cream, a box of graham crackers and a roll of sausage. Whatever she craved, he satisfied.

I couldn't even imagine being taken care of in such a way. I was lucky if Lee had bought me a beer at the beach. I asked God to show me where he was. But God didn't answer that prayer the way I wanted. I heard nothing from Lee. I called him numerous times with no response. I even called his mother, trying to track him down. I wondered if he had moved out of New York. All I knew was that he was gone. He knew about the baby. How could he not care if he had a son or daughter? I couldn't understand. He must be in denial. And, of course, fear. I made myself believe it was fear. Because if I went deeper, to the truth that he really didn't love me, or even care, the rejection would wreck me. It was more pain than I could bear.

With all the time I spent *thinking* in my bed the night before, I forgot to set my alarm. I woke up on my own at 8:10. My train left at 8:15. Shoot. *I'm gonna be late again.* I peeled myself out of bed. I thought about calling in sick, but I had just missed a week of work. Kim checked me out on Friday and gave me the okay to go back to work. So I got up, skipped my shower, put my hair up, and pulled a long, navy tent dress over my big belly.

After getting over the initial shock, my mom and dad called to talk to me. My mom didn't say a whole lot. But a week later I received a parcel from UPS. She filled a box with the most professional and attractive maternity clothes I could imagine. They were perfect for work. That was her way of accepting the news of the baby. I was so grateful for the clothes. The blue dress was one of my favorites. The material was soft, and it flowed nicely over my belly.

I made it to the station in time for the 8:50 train. I would be late, but I would make it. The train was running late. I paced up and down on the platform. At 9:05 it came rolling in. Plenty of empty seats were left. I took one by the window. There were five more stops before we ended at Grand Central. With each stop the train filled. My body was overflowing in my seat. I hoped no one sat next to me. But by stop number three most of the seats were taken, and a tall, attractive man in his twenties started to sit down next to me.

Feeling self-conscious, I buried my head in the *Daily News.*

"Mind if I sit here?" he asked with a Southern drawl.

"Sure, go ahead," I said.

He sat down, and I glanced at him from the corner of my eye. He was muscular and had a nice tan. His eyes were hazel, and he had a friendly smile. He caught me looking at him, and I wanted to hide. He kept looking at me, smiling, and then almost saying something but didn't.

I wanted to say, "Stop it! You're too cute, and I'm an elephant. Quit looking at me."

But I kept my mouth shut.

He looked again, and this time he spoke. "I'm sorry to bother you, miss, but I have to say, you are a beautiful woman."

I stared at him in disbelief. Did he just say that? He couldn't be a New Yorker. They don't do that kind of thing. I went back to reading my paper. He looked at me and smiled. I couldn't take it any longer. "Where are you from?" I asked.

"Raleigh, North Carolina," he said in that cute drawl.

"Really," I said.

"Yes, ma'am. Out here for a job interview. First time in the city."

That explained it.

"My name is Kurt," he said, reaching out his hand to shake mine.

"Hi, Kurt, I'm Grace."

"Good to meet you, Grace," and he kissed my hand.

I pulled my hand back in surprise. He sensed my anxiety. "Are all New Yorkers hardened and cold?"

"We are cold until we get to know you, and then we'll have your back no matter what."

"Where I am from, everyone's so friendly. This will be hard to get used to."

"Once you make a friend with a New Yorker," I said, "you will have a friend for life."

"Well, I reckon so, beautiful lady." He smiled his perfect smile at me.

I blushed. I had not felt beautiful in a long time. And here I was, almost nine months pregnant, and some Southern boy on the Metro was calling me beautiful. It made me giggle.

"What's so funny?" he asked.

"Oh, nothing, I just don't feel too beautiful right now," I confessed.

"Well, you most certainly are!" he said. "Your husband should tell you every day."

I couldn't bear to tell him I didn't have a husband. So I just smiled.

Patrick was supposed to be my husband. But alcohol and drugs were more beautiful to him than I was. I wrestled with my worth after he left. I struggled with the word "beautiful." I knew what it meant but never equated it with myself. As a young girl, I was tall, skinny, and had a long face like my long hair. The boys would call me "horse face." As I got older, it changed to "pizza face," because I had severe acne. I was teased constantly. I was so shy and insecure. Moving to a new city every two years didn't help my self-esteem either. I was always the new girl. It was hard for me to make friends, and I never felt like I fit in.

By the sixth grade I was five foot one and weighed one hundred pounds. I remember the day in class where we had to be weighed and measured for some fitness test. My petite friends ran up to the front of the room and jumped on the scale. Mr. Nyfler, my teacher, would read the number out loud for the nurse to record. "Sixty-five pounds, four foot six," he said. No one weighed more than seventy. Not even some of the boys.

Then it was my turn. I was mortified. I slunk up to the front of the room, hunched over. I stepped on the scale. All the kids watched. And then Mr. Nyfler did the kindest thing ever. He bent over and whispered in my ear, "One hundred. Five foot one. Now go tell the nurse."

I grinned big, jumped off the scale, and tiptoed to the nurse, whispering the information into her ear.

He saved me. Saved me from public humiliation at the age of twelve. I felt ashamed that I weighed more, but at least it was our secret.

That one act of kindness stayed with me for years. Through my teens my mom would scold, "Stand up straight, pull your belly in, and turn your feet out—walk straight." The words, said over and over again, gave me the message that I wasn't good enough. Not acceptable—definitely not beautiful. I felt ugly and awkward. God made a mistake when He made my body. My mom tried to fix me for years, but it never worked. I still hunched over. My feet turned in when I walked, and I had a little belly.

I sat on the train that morning with my belly out to there, hair in a non-Vogue ponytail, pimples on my chin. And now a cute, Southern boy called me *beautiful*.

And the best part of all, he wasn't trying to get into my pants.

CHAPTER 27

"**S**urprise!" shouted a group of my co-workers. They were gathered around a long table in one of the conference rooms. Pastel pink and blue balloons floated up close to the ceiling.

I jumped, but I was more surprised by my coworkers' caring than their shouting. I didn't think anyone here at work cared if I was having a baby or not, except for Jason, of course. And a few other female co-workers. But more than fifty people were in the room. It was standing room only. Rattles were tied to the balloon strings and dangling over the table. Packs of disposable diapers were stacked high in the corner like a pyramid.

In the center of the table was a large cake in the shape of an old-fashioned baby carriage. It was covered in sprinkles and white coconut.

"Do you like it?" asked Margo. She pranced up to me in her high heels. "I designed the cake."

"Really?" I said, not believing. She was into this whole baby shower thing.

Jason snuck up behind me and placed his hand on my back. "Only thirty-five minutes late," he said. "Not too bad."

"Hey, that's not fair! I didn't know they were doing this for me. I forgot to set my alarm and missed my train."

"Well, a lot more people were here, but sales had to go. Meetings called."

I felt bad. I was late for my own surprise baby shower. I tried not to let the guilt get the best of me. But that feeling of unworthiness came swooping back in.

Jason took my hand. "Let me lead you to your throne, your highness," he joked.

At the head of the table, Margo had wrapped a black leather chair in pink tissue paper and stenciled the word "Mommy" in big blue letters on the back of the chair.

Jason squinted. "It's a lot of pink."

"This is amazing. Margo really went all out," I said.

"I think she is trying to make it up to you, Grace," he said. "She wasn't too supportive in the beginning."

"Something has changed with her."

I sat down in my throne, trying not to tear the tissue paper. People huddled in groups, drinking pink punch.

"Okay! Everyone find a seat!" shouted Margo. "It's time for presents."

"Aw, what about the cake?" said Bill from the mail room. "I came for the cake."

I turned to see Bill grabbing a fork. I was surprised he was here. Gifts were passed down to me. I opened one baby item after another. Onesies, receiving blankets, sleepers, and baby toys. Tiny socks and baby shoes. I was overwhelmed that they did all this for me.

The women oohed and awed. "That's so cute!" must have been said a hundred times. The men, however, stared in boredom and ate all the baby-bottle-shaped cookies. One giant gift was sitting in the back. Two men had to carry it over to me.

"What in the world. . . ?" I asked.

"Just open it!" said Margo. She sounded like a five-year-old at a birthday party.

I ripped off the baby-footprint paper and tried to find the up end of this huge box.

Bill handed me scissors, and I sliced open the top of the box. Inside were shiny metal parts. I pulled out a piece trying to figure out what it was. Margo was getting impatient and finally blurted out, "It's a swing! A baby swing!"

"Wow!" was all I could say.

She helped me take out the pieces, and Bill from the mailroom with the help of John from accounting put it together in less than five minutes.

"It's really a swing," I said. "Margo, thank you so much! I love it!"

I was so excited. But not too sure how I was going to get it home on the train. Margo interrupted my thoughts. "I was reading how babies love the motion of the swinging. It simulates being in the womb and is really soothing."

"Okay, then. You read that, too?" I said.

"There's a lot of information out there. I spent some time in the library too. I've learned quite a bit," she said.

People laughed and ate pink cake. Then one by one they said their good-byes and gave me helpful baby tips. Many had to make quick exits to get to their meetings. I was just amazed they came.

Jason, Margo, and I were the last three in the room. We were working on our second pieces of cake.

"This is good stuff," said Jason. "Where did you get this?" he asked Margo.

"I made it," she said.

"You made this?" I asked in shock.

"Yeah. There's more to me than you know," she quipped.

"Yes, there is. I can't believe you made this." I stuffed another bite in my mouth.

"Well, just because you don't believe in something, doesn't mean it isn't true."

Her eyes met mine and stayed there a little longer than normal. "I'm sorry I didn't believe you in the beginning."

"In the beginning?" I asked.

"Yeah, when I said it was a mass of tissue and not a baby," she confessed.

"Oh, that," I said.

"I guess I didn't want to believe it. It was easier not to."

"Why is that?" I asked.

"Because the truth was too painful. It was easier to believe the lie," she said.

"I know what you mean," I said. "I didn't want to believe it either. I denied it in the very beginning and wanted it to go away."

"But you didn't," she said. "You are brave. Braver than I was."

"Brave?" I said. "I don't know if I'd call it brave. I fell apart, and the doctor couldn't do it."

"I know," she said. "That's what makes you brave. A lot of women can deny it. They can terminate their pregnancy without anyone ever knowing. But you're different. You're going through with it. I could never do what you are doing."

"It's not easy. Doing it alone. But you could do it if you had to," I said.

"No, I couldn't. I didn't." Her eyes welled up with tears.

I got up, grabbed some tissues, and went to sit down next to Margo.

"Here you go," I said as I handed her a tissue. I put my arm around her and whispered in her ear. "I think you are brave, Margo. You don't have to go through this alone." Her cries got stronger. "We all do the best we can, and sometimes we make mistakes. But God still loves you. He forgives you."

"I hope so," Margo said.

"Take it from someone who knows. He does," I said. "There is healing in forgiveness. Let the shame go."

Margo hugged me and gave me a small smile. "Thank you," she said. "For listening."

"Anytime."

Jason broke the seriousness of the moment. "Hey, preggo! You're not alone. I'm your Lamaze partner, or did you forget?"

"Lamaze partner?" blurted Margo. "He's your Lamaze partner?" Her sad tears were now turning into happy ones as she laughed at Jason.

"Yes, I am," Jason said. "And a darn good one."

"Yes, and you will probably hear jokes about it down at the comedy club in the Village," I said. "So he's getting something out of this."

"You be nice, preggo. Or no ice chips for you!"

CHAPTER 28

Mother's Day was coming fast. But I felt as if I would never be a mother. I was ten days past my due date. I still came into work every day, which made my coworkers nervous, but I did not know what else to do. I had cleaned the bassinette and changing table several times, scrubbed the hardwood floors, and washed all my linens. Sheila popped down the stairs at least two or three times per week to check on me.

"Any progress?" she asked.

"Nothing," I'd answer in defeat.

I was big as a house, weighing in at 203. I'd gained more than the recommended thirty-five pounds. The late nights of ice cream binges helped me add an extra fifteen on top. But I didn't care. I just wanted this baby out. I wanted to see my feet, put on shoes, and not have to pee every ten minutes.

I lumbered into the city on a sunny Thursday. It was so warm that I didn't even need a coat. I took the day off of work to visit my midwife downtown at Saint Vincent's Hospital. She wanted to give me a stress test and see how the baby was doing.

I wore long, cutoff denim shorts I handmade from my maternity jeans with the elastic waist. That was the one casual item my mom thoughtfully packed in her care package. I lived in those jeans every weekend. Now they were shorts. Spring was in full bloom, and the humidity was rising into the sweat zone. I found a long, oversized blouse to wear over my new shorts. It had a beachy print with sail boats and flowers and reminded me of the ocean. I had not been out to the beach since the day I conceived this child with Lee. I'd given up on him. He would not return my phone calls. His mom had even hung up on me. I wish I had his social security number. Since he worked construction under the table, it would be difficult to find him to get child support. I needed more information, but it appeared that he had vanished from the planet.

Jason was wonderful. He was eager and ready to take his post by my side at the top of the bed and help me breathe. Since my due date, May 10, he had called me every night.

"Anything yet, preggo?"

"No, not yet," I said.

"Hang in there. He or she will come out when they're ready," he said.

Jason was convinced it was a boy, but I thought it was a girl. I was also excited at the thought of a daughter. The ultrasound was blurry, and we didn't have a clear view of the baby.

I slipped on my sandals and left the apartment with nothing but a small leather shoulder bag holding the essentials: keys, tokens, a few dollars, and my lipstick.

I took my time walking to the train. I chose the subway from 205th Street that day, even though it was a longer ride than the Metro north commuter train. The 4 train made at least seven stops in the Bronx before crossing into Manhattan at 102nd Street.

I sat, enjoying the ride, rocking back and forth with the motion of the train, grateful for the time alone. Two more stops to Grand Central. I prepared to exit and catch the 6 train down to the Village. I loved going into the Village. The artists, musicians, and hippies gathered and lived there. A young girl in all black wearing a bright orange beret stepped on at Bleeker Street. Her ebony hair shone from under the orange wool. She looked like a painter from Soho. I liked to imagine the lives of the artists I would encounter in the Village. Sipping coffee in the Bleeker den, playing guitar in Washington Street Park, or perhaps reciting poetry in a West Village loft. I wanted to be a Village person, immersed in art, culture, and spirited freedom.

A kick in my ribs interrupted my daydream. I placed my hand on my belly, patting softly, coaxing my baby to calmness. "We're almost there," I whispered.

The scent of rosemary blended with oregano floated in the hot air, hovering around the bodega on the corner of 19th and Seventh Avenue. It smelled sweet and spicy and enticed me to stop in the Italian deli and see what was cooking. The little deli was bustling with people ordering their lunches. The bubbling hot pasta sauce filled the place with warmth. I settled on a slice of toasted Italian bread with melted mozzarella and a dapple of spicy red sauce. *Maybe this will get the baby going.* I grabbed a cold lemonade from the freezer case and paid the young boy at the counter. He smiled at me and said, "Beautiful," as he handed me my change. I blushed, took my bread and lemonade and headed out to enjoy the sun. I crossed the street to go sit in Washington Square Park.

The park was full of life and movement. A teenage boy was dancing near his boom box. A group of older guys played cards.

Another man walked around conspicuously in red velvet pants standing tall on stilts. The music was loud, and so were the people talking and laughing. In the corner an old man set up books on a card table with a green sign that said, "For sale." Girls gathered by a vendor selling handmade jewelry and handbags.

I loved it here in the park. The creative energy inspired me, and I could be whoever I wanted. Anything could happen in Washington Square.

I sat on the edge of the stone fountain and sipped my bottled lemonade. Time stopped as the sun's rays caressed the bare skin on my arms and legs. I watched a middle-age woman standing at the wooden easel, painting the street scene she saw in her view.

How I wished I could paint, sing, or draw. I loved to write. When the other girls were playing dolls in third grade, I would play at writing. Play writing was my favorite game with my best friend Becky. We would sit for hours in silence, each in our own corner of the bedroom. We wrote stories with fat, pastel markers. When our stories were done, we would switch notebooks and read the other's creation.

The desire to write stories drew me to the city. To the Village, into the world of art and romance. I wanted the artist's life. To create and be a part of the creation. Instead I ended up trapped in a corner cubicle editing promotional copy and scheduling commercials. Nothing was being created. Only packaged and sold. I had settled.

Security and mediocrity held me captive. No risk, but no romance either. I admired the courage of artists who dared to come to this place, leaving all the security of home behind. Coming to create, to live among the other free-spirited gypsies. Selling their creations on the street. No doubt some made it big, landing a show in Soho or selling a story to one of the Madison Avenue publishing houses.

But what about the others? Were they still waiting for their break? They were faithful, showing up every day, setting up shop in the streets. I desired to have their tenacity and courage.

I wished I could be so brave.

The chimes from a nearby church counted up the hours. I had lost track of the time and was late for my three o'clock appointment. I stood up, stretched, and made myself leave the park.

CHAPTER 29

A stained glass cross hung suspended over the double doors of the hospital entrance. The sun shone through the glass, illuminating the red, gold, and sea blue.

Upon entering, I was greeted by a young girl in a pinstriped dress. "May I direct you to your floor?" she asked.

"Labor and delivery." I said.

"Oh, my! Do you need a wheelchair? Who are you with?" She became frantic and tried to rush me to the elevator.

"No, I'm fine. I'm not in labor yet. I'm just here for some test," I said, trying to reassure her.

Her posture relaxed. "Oh, good. This is my first day, and I've never escorted a pregnant mom to delivery."

"Unfortunately for me, this baby is not in any hurry to arrive."

She led me to the elevator and pressed the button for me. "Good luck," she said, as the door shut.

As the door opened, women were pacing the halls, breathing hard, and men were following them rubbing their backs. One woman paused to rest, bend over, and let out a painful groan. The noise startled me and made my heart skip a beat.

I found my way to the nurse's station, my heart beating rapidly. "I'm here for a stress test," I said. Seeing these women in labor made my stress level increase. I hoped I would pass the test.

"Have a seat," she said. "Someone will call you in a few minutes."

I sat in the lounge, closed my eyes, and tried to get my heart to slow down. But all I could see was the agony on that woman's face. That pain looked real. This was all too real.

I knew I wasn't ready. I tried my deep breathing, but it didn't help. The nurse finally called my name after what felt like an hour. I followed her to an exam room.

"Put this on, open in the back. The doctor will be in, in a moment," the nurse said.

"But wait. Where's Kim? My midwife?" I asked, confused.

"She's not doing the test. She's not in the hospital today. Dr. Concordia will be seeing you. He'll be right in," said the nurse.

My pulse increased. Who was Dr. Concordia? I wanted Kim.

The doctor entered in a whirlwind, full of energy and agitation. He studied my chart, even before greeting me. "Grace?" he asked. "I'm Dr. Concordia. I'll be doing the stress test."

"Where is Kim?" I asked.

"She's not here today. Don't you worry. We all work as a team. I've got this," he reassured me. "It looks like you're a little overdue. Going on forty-one weeks?"

"Yes," I said. "Is that bad?"

"Well, let's take a look and see what's going on here." He had me lie back and scoot down. I was at the end of the table, legs wide open.

"You are not progressing as well as we hoped," he said. "You are effaced, but only dilated to two centimeters. Not much change from two weeks ago." He frowned.

"Kim said that was normal. I could be at two for weeks, and the baby would come when she was ready," I argued.

"True, true, but we need to make sure the baby is still getting what it needs and it's not under stress." He looked concerned.

Two nurses came in the room, rolling in a machine. They hooked wires up to my heart and to my belly. The doctor left the room while they ran the test. Fifteen minutes later he came back in to take a look at the printout and image on the screen.

"Hmm," he said. It didn't sound promising. "Grace, I'm afraid you are leaking amniotic fluid. And that's not good for the baby."

I felt fine. I thought everything was fine. Now he was afraid. That made me afraid. "I don't know what you mean."

"If you lose too much fluid, your baby will be in distress," he said. "The best thing we can do right now is admit you and induce labor before it gets any worse."

"Admit me? Induce labor?" I asked. "This was not the plan. I planned a natural childbirth. No drugs, no inducing. Just my midwife and Jason, with the breathing."

"I know, but sometimes plans have to change. The first one out can take a little coaxing," he said. First one? He was already planning more babies for me, and I just wanted to let this one come out on her own. I wasn't prepared for the plans to change now. "We need to get things started, and then the baby will do the rest," he said.

I did not like the sound of it. They were admitting me, putting a plastic bracelet on my wrist and hooking me up to a machine to monitor my vitals and another one for my contractions. I wasn't ready. I didn't have my birthing bag with all my essentials. I needed my breathing cue sheet, my music, my clock, and my socks.

The hospital room was cold and sterile. I needed my visual focal point. My picture. I needed Jason or Sheila. I needed my mom.

But I had no one and nothing. I was alone. Alone with this baby, who didn't want to come out. And I wasn't ready for it to come out either. This was not how it was supposed to go.

My agitation stressed my body and elevated my blood pressure. The nurse kept telling me to relax and breathe. But I couldn't breathe or relax without my plan.

They let me make a few phone calls. I called Michelle at work and got her voice mail. Next I tried Sheila, but there was no answer. I wanted to call Jason, but the nurse made me lie back so she could take my blood pressure again.

My pulse was eighty, far above my normal resting heart rate of sixty-four.

"Try to relax," the nurse pleaded. "This isn't good for the baby or you."

I shut my eyes and decided to pray. "Please, God, help me. Send somebody. I can't do this alone. I'm not ready."

Tears rolled down the side of my face. I let out a stifled cry just as the phone rang by my bed. It didn't register in my brain that it was for me. By the fourth ring, the nurse asked, "Do you want me to answer that?"

Opening my eyes, I cried, "Yes!"

She handed me the receiver.

"Hello," I said, in a cracking voice.

"Gracie, it's me, Sheila. Are you in labor? Michelle got your message at work and rang me straight away," she said.

"Sheila, thank God! Yes, I'm at Saint Vincent's downtown already."

"I thought that was just the test?" she asked.

"I know. But I'm leaking fluid. They're inducing me. I don't know what to do."

"Don't worry one wee bit," she said. "Bryan will be home by four. I will take the train and be right down."

"My bag, I need my birthing bag."

"Is it packed?"

"A little. I didn't put everything in yet. I thought there was time."

"Don't you worry. I'll get it from Michelle."

"Okay, don't forget the focal point, my music CD, oh, and the stop-clock thingy. And bring the outfits for the baby. They are on the changing table."

My first contraction hit. And my mind forgot what else was on my list.

"Gracie, you all right?" Sheila asked.

They had started a drip of Pitocin, and the contractions were starting. Ready or not.

"Please hurry," I said.

"My dear, I will get everything. Don't you worry. Remember your breathing. You're going to see your wee baby soon. She's coming."

The nurse put the receiver back on the hook. I tried to breathe through the pain. "Hee, hee, shee, shee," I said with each breath.

I sounded like a snake in cardiac arrest.

"You're doing great," the nurse said. "Almost through it."

She watched a screen where a crooked line zigged up and down measuring the size and length of each contraction. The screen said it was over, but the pain in my belly told me it was just beginning.

Jason got the message from Michelle. But I didn't know when he would be on his way. For the next few hours I labored alone with Pitocin dripping into my veins. Between contractions I tried to obey the orders to rest, but my mind wouldn't let me. It was close to six, and still no one was here. I was cold and alone.

Finally, at about 6:45, a familiar face popped into my room. It was Michelle, still in her suit, coming up from Wall Street. I wasn't sure she'd be able to handle the birthing part but was so relieved to see her.

"Mish! You're here! It's happening. Today," I said.

"I know. I can see that." She eyed all the machines. "What's with all the wires? I thought you were going to do it the natural way," she joked.

"Yeah, well, plans change," I said.

"You okay?"

"Do I look okay?" I said as I breathed through another contraction.

Michelle's sarcastic humor was a welcome relief to my pain. She made me laugh even in labor. "You have enough drugs here?"

"No, they're not pain drugs. It's Pitocin to induce the labor. I want to protect the baby. No drugs."

"Yeah! Forget the baby! You look awful. I think you need drugs."

"Kim said I could do this with my Lamaze breathing," I argued.

"Lamaze breathing sounds more like hyperventilating. And where's Kim anyway? Isn't she supposed to be here for this part?" she said, laughing.

"I don't know. Probably at the birthing center. Where I was supposed to be having this baby, in the blue room."

"It doesn't look like you're going anywhere soon," she said. "Better get used to the gray room." She laughed. "Jeez, what is all this hardware? You having a baby or a heart attack?"

I didn't laugh this time. Another contraction was building. "Shee, shee, sha, sha."

"You hold that thought," she said. "I'll be right back." And she left the room.

I'd been laboring for four hours but still was only dilated to three centimeters. They increased the Pitocin to strengthen my contractions. I thought they were strong enough before. By then, Michelle had found Jason and Sheila. All three of them were there, taking turns giving me ice chips and helping me breathe. Michelle and Jason provided comic relief, making jokes about my appearance and snapping photos with the camera.

In haste to get my birthing bag together, Sheila and Michelle had grabbed whatever they could find. Instead of socks, they packed bright pink leg warmers. So my feet were freezing, but my calves were toasty warm. It made for quite a picture with my light blue hospital gown.

I did have my focal point—a picture of a beach. My breathing instructions were there, printed on a white piece of parchment paper. But they couldn't find the stop watch and instead snagged the kitchen clock off the wall. I had this giant, round clock propped up at the end of the bed so we could watch the second hand measure the contractions.

They couldn't find my music, so Jason hummed songs from the 70s to me and did his best impression of Barry White.

I didn't care that I was wearing pink leg warmers and staring at a giant kitchen clock in my bed. I was just happy they were all there and I wasn't alone.

The seconds ticked into minutes and the minutes into hours. This baby did not want to come out. This child was stubborn.

Kim finally made it in around ten. She had already brought two lives into the world that day and was ready for baby number three. I felt relieved to see her and gave her a long-winded account of what these doctors had done to me. She assured me that all was well and that even with the best intentions and plans for a natural childbirth, things can happen and we must change our course.

By now my water had broken entirely, and the baby needed to move on out. Kim called a conference in the hall with the labor nurses and doctor. "Her labor isn't progressing; the baby's heart rate is stable. I think we need to back off on the Pitocin and let her rest through the night and start again in the morning," she said. The doctor didn't agree and wanted to press on.

They agreed to stop the Pitocin at midnight and see if the contractions would continue on their own. If not, they would monitor me and the baby and let me get five or six hours of sleep.

Midnight came. And the Pitocin and labor stopped. I was mentally and physically exhausted. Thinking the baby wasn't coming tonight, I told my clan to go home and sleep. Michelle and Sheila stepped in to say good night and said they would be back by seven in the morning. But Jason did not want to leave me. Kim said she could find him an empty bed.

She left and said she would come back to check on me in an hour. "Get some sleep. Tomorrow's a busy day."

Once again I was alone, in the dark, sterile room. I was too sleepy to care. The only sounds I could hear were the swishing noise of the sonogram machine and the baby's heartbeat.

CHAPTER 30

"You gonna have this baby today or what?" asked Michelle. "I got things to do." Michelle's perky voice and bright blue eyes woke me from my sleep.

"Where am I?" I asked, forgetting for a moment.

"Umm, Gracie, you're in the hospital, having a baby. You sure they're not pumping drugs into you with this drip thing?"

"What time is it?"

"What? You can't see our giant kitchen clock from there?" she joked. "It's time to push this thing out!"

I had slept a good six hours with no contractions. "I don't think this little one wants to come out yet," I said, rubbing my swollen belly.

"You tell him to get a move-on! I got places to go, things to do. By the way, nice leg warmers! You may set a new trend in labor wear." She laughed.

"Hey, you're the one who packed them and forgot the socks!"

"Don't blame me," she said. "I don't know anything about baby paraphernalia. It was Sheila."

"Speaking of Sheila, where is she?" I asked.

"She said she'd be back this morning. She had to find a sitter for all those rug rats of hers."

"And Jason?" I asked.

"Oh, your birthing husband?" she joked. "I think he's in the dining room hitting on some nurse."

"Stop it!" I said. But I couldn't stop laughing.

"Focus now," she said. "You need to get back to that breathing thing and get this baby out." She stepped to the end of the bed to set up my focal point and kitchen clock.

"Can you see this from there? I think you may need a bigger clock."

"That's the only one Sheila could find with a second hand," I said in Sheila's defense.

"Well, I'm glad she was able to find our kitchen clock. When you're done here, do ya think she could bring it back and hang it on the wall?"

We laughed hard together. It felt good to have my best friend back. Even though it was hard for Michelle to express sentimental emotion, I knew she loved me.

"Hey, I'll check in with you later, 'K? Let me know if there's anything else you need, maybe our kitchen table? To set your clock on?"

"Get out of here!" I exclaimed. "Go to work. I'm fine."

She leaned over me and pressed her ear to my belly. "Don't hear much going on in there. Are you sure she's in there?"

"Hey, you need to come out of there," she said to the baby bump. "We want to meet you. And wait till you see your mom." She looked at me and made a scary face. "You're gonna scare her with those pink leg warmers."

"You need to go!" I said. "I will call you if anything happens."

"Okay, I won't hold my breath," she said. "See ya."

I felt stronger today. The sleep did me good. I finally let go and surrendered to this process, even though it wasn't my plan. I looked up to the sky to talk to God.

"Okay, God," I said. "I'm ready for Your plan. Help me do this."

I felt a warmth wash over me, and somehow I knew He heard my voice.

Dr. Concordia came in at 10:30 in the morning all business like. "Glad to see you awake," he said. "Let's have a baby today. What do ya say?" He winked at me.

"I'm ready if she is," I said.

"So you know it's a girl?" he asked.

"The sonogram wasn't clear, but Kim is sure it's a girl," I said smiling.

He checked me and the baby, and things looked all right. But I was still only at three centimeters. He wanted to start the Pitocin again to get things going. At this point I was in no mood to argue. The slow drip entered my veins, and soon I was counting the minutes as the contractions came. I stared at my paper ocean view, breathed in and out with my "hee, hee" breathing, and gently tried to talk this baby out of its warm womb.

Jason came back after grabbing some breakfast and started his joking and coaching again. The nurse suggested a lap around the floor to help move things along. So Jason carried my ice chips and pushed my machine as I circled the floor in my blue gown and pink leg warmers.

Two hours later another progress check. I was now at five centimeters. My contractions were regular and strong. Dr. Concordia stopped the Pitocin drip and let me and the baby go on our own. About every hour he or Kim would come in to check my progress, as if they were checking a roast in the oven. "Is it done yet?" A poke here, a poke there. Check the temperature. "No, not yet. Another thirty minutes."

I breathed. I walked. I squatted. I moaned.

CHAPTER 31

"No baby yet," I told Sheila when she got back into the room. "But it hurts like—." I couldn't finish my sentence because another contraction was starting right on top of the last one. Sheila's mothering instincts kicked into gear. She fluffed my pillows, massaged my lower back, and fed me an ice chip after each contraction. When the pain got really bad she rubbed my forehead, smoothing back my hair.

"This baby is coming, you know," she said. "Won't be long now."

"I know," was all I could say. The pain was too intense to talk.

"Here comes another one, me dear," she said in her sweet Irish voice. "Deep breaths, you're almost through it. Just one more breath."

The contractions were now coming a lot closer together with barely any time in between to rest. "I can't do this anymore!" I cried. "It's too much. . .the pain is too much. I need drugs! Give me drugs!" I yelled.

"Hush, hush, my dear," Sheila said. "You'll be fine. You're doing great."

"No, I can't!" I cried.

"Hold on. I'll get the doctor and see what he can give you."

"No, don't leave me," I pleaded.

"I'll be right back. Don't ya worry," she said.

But I was worried. Worried I couldn't do this. Worried the baby was stuck.

Dr. Concordia came in for his hourly check. He confirmed my worry. The baby's heart rate was falling. It wasn't good.

"She's at seven," he told the nurse. He talked to the nurse in code, like I wasn't even there. Did he not see me? I desperately needed to know what was going on, but no one would talk. Finally he looked at me. His face was serious. He glanced at the machine monitoring my vitals. "Your blood pressure is up. I think it's time to give you something for the pain," he said. I was too out of it to discuss the matter. He leaned over to the nurse. "Let's try an epidural," he said. "Grace, we are going to give you an epidural, okay? Dr. Davis, one of our interns, will be administering it. We are a teaching hospital. Is that okay with you?"

"I guess," I mumbled.

The bedside phone started to ring. I picked it up on the seventh ring. "Hey, girl? You still pregnant?" Jason said.

"Jason! Where are you? You need to be here."

"I know, I know. I got stuck in midtown traffic, but I'm on my way. Hang in there, preggo," he said.

"Gotta go. . .another one is coming." I dropped the phone to get through the contraction. Stabbing pain shot through my lower back and deep into my pelvis. I felt nauseous and couldn't control my breathing. Instead of "hee, shees," deep moans came from my belly. About five contractions later, Jason swept through the door. He was carrying a bottle of water and fresh flowers.

"I'm here," he said. "Remember your breathing." He tried to encourage me.

But I was done. I lay on my side, clutching the edge of the bed. He slid behind me and put pressure on my low back with both hands. "You can do this, Gracie," he said in a whisper.

The contraction subsided, and I let out a deep exhale followed by a flow of tears.

"What's this?" he asked. "No crying yet," he teased.

"I'm sorry. It's just so hard, and I'm exhausted."

"Is Sheila here?"

"Yes. She's here somewhere. I think she went to find Kim."

"Well, I'm here now for the duration. Not going anywhere," he said. "It's me and you, kid."

"Thank God," I said. "This is more work than I thought it would be. No one tells you."

"I think that is why they call it labor," said Jason.

"Ha ha, cute. Quit being a smart aleck and give me some ice. Ohh, here comes another one."

"It's okay," he said. "I've got you. Focus, focus on the ocean."

I squeezed my eyes shut, trying to see my beach. At first it was comforting, but then it reminded me of Lee, and I was infuriated. He was probably out in the wild blue, catching a wave without a care in the world. I hated him for doing this to me. He had brought me so much pain. It wasn't fair.

"This is Dr. Davis," Dr. Concordia said. "He's a first-year intern and will be giving you the epidural."

I stared at Dr. Davis. He looked about twenty-seven, just a few years older than me.

"Are you going to stay in here for the procedure?" Jason asked Dr. Concordia.

"Yes, I'll be right here, walking him through every step," he said. "We'll wait till after your next contraction."

Jason got me through the next one. I held on to his arm so tight it left red marks. He moved in front of me while the doctor got me ready for the needle. I felt my gown being untied and slipped open. Dr. Davis rubbed a cold alcohol-smelling liquid on my spine. I didn't look at the needle, but later Jason told me it was very long. I just stared at Jason's face and held his hand.

I felt a pinch. That was the novocaine. Then a few minutes later the needle slid into my spinal column. They told me to lie very still, even though my whole body was vibrating in pain. But I did my best. I felt pressure pushing into my spine. Then a little tingling pain, but nothing compared to what I'd been going through.

"A little more," said Dr. Concordia. "There, you got it. Now slowly pull the needle out," he instructed.

He did it. Or so I thought.

I turned over and waited for the magic to begin. I was supposed to be numb from the waist down. Fifteen minutes later my left side was totally numb, but I could feel everything, even more intensely, on my right side.

"Great," I said to Jason. "He messed up."

"Should I call them back?"

"No, no more needles. I'll deal."

I felt intense pain on one side of my body and nothing on the other side. I didn't like the feeling of having no feeling. It made me feel even more out of control. For the next few hours we labored. Me, Jason, and Sheila. Kim showed up around five to check on me. She wasn't happy about the epidural and my progress, but it was done. She felt sad that my natural birthing plan was thrown out the window, but she stayed positive and encouraged me.

"Want me to check your cervix again?" she asked.

"Yes! Please tell me I'm at ten and I can push," I pleaded.

Jason stepped up to the head of the bed as Kim peered and poked.

"Not quite a ten yet, but a good solid eight," she said.

"Eight," I groaned. "I've labored all this time and only opened one more centimeter?" I buried my head in my soggy pillow. "I quit."

"You can't quit," Jason said in my ear. "You are almost there."

Dr. Concordia popped back in to check on my progress.

"I just checked her," Kim said. "She's an eight."

"Good girl," he said. "We're getting there."

He left as quickly as he came in, almost running over Michelle at the door to my room.

"I'm back," said Michelle. "What'd I miss?"

Before I could answer, the machine monitoring the baby's heart rate started to beep. Two seconds later a team of nurses rushed in to find out what was wrong. At a frantic pace they moved the wires attached to my belly.

"What's wrong?" I asked. But no one answered me.

"What's happening?" Jason asked.

"Page Dr. Concordia," said one of the nurses.

"Please tell us what is going on here," Jason said.

Finally the nurse looked at me. "We lost the baby's heartbeat."

"What?" I asked, not believing her words. "You lost it?"

"Lay back, honey. Just breathe. We'll get it back," she said.

She laid the scope on my belly and moved it around like she was chasing a hockey puck. She stopped suddenly. "Here it is. We got it. But it's weak."

Another contraction pierced through my middle. "Jason!" I yelled.

"I'm here. I'm here." He breathed with me through the entire contraction.

The nurse looked confused. "You still feeling pain?" she asked. "I thought you got the epidural?"

"She did," Jason said. "But it only took on one side of her body."

The nurse didn't respond.

Michelle handed me the ice chips. "That was a doozy, huh?"

"You have no idea," I said. "I am never, ever doing this again."

"Oh, that's what every woman says," Sheila said. "But when you hold your wee baby in your arms for the first time, you'll forget about all the pain."

"Fat chance," I said. "I'll never forget."

Michelle gave Sheila a disgusted look. "And you did this four times?"

"Yes, four lovely wee ones," Sheila said.

"You can have one more for me, 'cuz I ain't ever having kids," Michelle said.

Sheila pulled out my camera. "Go stand next to Mama," she told Michelle.

"No more pictures," I said. "I look terrible."

"Yeah, save some film for the kid," Michelle said.

"I have plenty," she said as she clicked the camera. The flash made me see spots.

"Someone, please take that camera away from her," I pleaded.

"Calm down, Mama. Here comes another one," Sheila said.

"The pain feels deeper. Is it time to push?" I asked.

"Get Kim!" Jason told Michelle.

"It must have been the camera," Sheila said. "She is ready for the spotlight. Wants her grand entrance to be captured on film."

Kim came in quickly and checked me out. "Guess what, Gracie?" She smiled.

"Better be good news," I said.

"You are ready to push," she said.

"Yes, thank God," I said.

"On your next contraction, okay," said Kim. "One, two, three, push!" she yelled.

I pushed and pushed, my face turning red, but it felt like nothing was moving.

"Okay, stop. Rest. We'll try again on the next one," Kim said.

Dr. Concordia came back in the room. "I heard there was some pushing going on in here," he said. He slipped on his rubber gloves and assisted Kim. "Let's sit you up a little," he said. Jason helped me up, and I took a deep breath.

"Okay, push!" the doctor ordered.

I pushed with all my might but again felt nothing move. "Is it coming?" I asked.

The doctor looked concerned. "The epidural makes it hard to push. You can't feel the sensation," he said. "But you are doing great."

Now I was getting agitated. I looked at Jason. "I didn't want the stupid epidural. It was their idea. Remember—I had the natural childbirth plan?" I said frustrated. "Now I can't even feel to push my baby out."

"Yeah," said Jason. "But you remember the pain?"

For the next thirty minutes I strained, pushed and groaned. But the baby was not moving. Sheila traded places with Jason to give him a break. He slipped out into the hall with Michelle.

The epidural was starting to wear off, but that was okay. It was easier to push.

Kim watched the monitor closely. "The baby's heart rate is going down again. She's in distress. Grace, we need you to change positions. The baby doesn't like this one," she said. "Let's get you on all fours." Sheila held my back and assisted as I got up on my hands and knees like a cat. It worked. The baby's heartbeat came up.

"Okay, Gracie, here we go again," Kim said. "Give me one big push."

This time I felt movement. I pushed through the pain, hoping she would pop right out. But she didn't.

"She's too tired," Kim said to the nurse.

"Grace, try to rest, okay? We will push again in a minute." So I stayed on all fours and pushed again. But the baby's heart rate went back down.

"We need to get this baby out," said the nurse. "I'm getting the doctor."

Dr. Concordia came in and took a look at the monitor. "Get the O.R. ready. We need to prep her for a C-section," he said with urgency.

"No!" I protested. "I can do it! Let me push again."

Kim tried to assist me, but her efforts weren't working. "Focus, Grace. We can do this."

I pleaded with God to help me get my baby out. I pushed once more with all my might, but she wasn't budging.

"We're going to move you now, Grace," said Dr. Concordia. They transferred me to a gurney and wheeled me down the hall. Doctors and nurses moved with fast-paced precision.

Frantic footsteps followed me to the O.R. "Only one person can come in with her," the nurse said. She looked at my panicked face lying on the bed. "Who will it be?" she asked. "Quick," she added.

Sheila. It had to be Sheila. She had done this four times. "Sheila," I said.

The nurse handed Sheila some scrubs, a mask and gloves. "Put these on," she said.

Sheila obeyed. Once the gloves were on, they wheeled me in under a bright light and draped my legs.

"Scalpel," I heard the doctor say. Between the flurry of the doctors and nurses, the bright light and frantic movement, I did not fully comprehend what was about to happen. I thought I needed to push again. The doctor started telling me what he was about to do. A six-inch cut at my bikini line. I was confused. Sheila was covered head-to-toe in light blue scrubs and had a white mask over her face.

When the doctor finished his instructions for the emergency C-section, he walked away for a second. Sheila, standing by my head, removed her mask and in her soothing Gaelic voice whispered in my ear, "Come on, Gracie. You can do this. Just try one more big push and you'll see your wee baby."

The epidural had totally worn off, and I could feel every sensation. The pain was off the charts. As the contraction reached its peak, I sat forward and gave it all I had. I pushed so hard that my scream echoed down the halls.

The doctor, back by my feet, scalpel in hand, saw the head. "The baby's crowning," he said. This news gave me the energy to push again. I had a burst of supernatural strength and pushed again. This time the fuzzy little head came out into the open. Sheila was so excited.

She yelled, "The head's out! The wee little head!"

"Hold it right there," the doctor said.

He suctioned out the baby's mouth and held the head in his hand. "One more push, to get the shoulders out." He used his hands to guide the shoulders and torso as I pushed one last time with a powerful, life-giving force.

She slid right into his arms. I felt the release and lay still in exhaustion. The doctor held her up for a moment. "Meet your baby girl," he said. I stared in awe. She was purple.

The nurse scooped up my baby, took her to the side, and started suctioning, wiping and weighing. And then I heard it. The loudest, most boisterous cry. Like she was saying, "I'm here! Hear me roar!"

"It's a wee baby girl," Sheila said, bursting with joy. "You did it, Mamma!"

"A girl?" I half asked and stated.

"A beautiful baby girl," the doctor said. They swaddled her in a blanket and laid her on my chest. I gazed into her dark blue eyes, and she looked straight into mine. We were connected. Even though I didn't recognize her looks, I completely knew her.

Her tiny bound-up body pressed against my heart. I could feel her warmth and see her crinkled little face. She lay on my chest for a few minutes, so quiet and content, gazing into my eyes, which were now flowing with tears.

All pain vanished. Only joy and love filled my being.

Sheila brushed my hair back, caressing my forehead. "You did it," she said. "You brought this life into the world. She's just precious."

After our brief introduction the nurse took her away to do her initial exam. The doctor started to press on my deflated belly, helping me birth the placenta. Although it wasn't pleasant, the pain was erased by my unspeakable joy. I couldn't wait to hold my precious baby in my arms again.

Once the placenta was safely out, the doctor wheeled me into the recovery room. I lost a lot of blood and had to be monitored closely. I lay there, alone, in a tiny room with only a curtain for a wall. Sheila left to go spread the good news of my new baby girl.

A peace rested on me like a warm blanket. I looked up to heaven. "Thank You, God," I said. "Thank You for saving my baby."

The curtain opened, and the nurse was there with my sweet baby girl. "Here's your daughter," she said. "She looks good. Scored a ten on the Apgar scale." She laid her on my chest, and I hugged one arm around her as I lay in recovery waiting for the bleeding to subside.

"Hi, there," I said. "I've been waiting for you." All I could do was grin and stare at her perfect little face. She didn't cry or wiggle. She lay on my chest, peaceful and content.

The sound of footsteps approached the recovery area. The nurse left the curtain open a little, and I could see a group of people walking toward me. It was a group of four couples, taking a tour of the birthing unit. A young male nurse led the group pointing and talking as they walked. "Over here is the recovery room, where new mothers often have to wait after giving birth," he said.

I felt four pairs of eyes stare at me lying on the gurney. I smiled back with pride. "I did it! See my baby girl! You can do it, too." They just stared at me. A couple of the women smiled back. And then they continued their tour.

I felt proud, strong and complete. My life was beginning anew. I could do anything.

Nothing was impossible with God.

CHAPTER 32

nvincible. That was how I felt. I brought a little human into the world. A tiny baby girl came out of me. It was more amazing than anyone could explain or fathom unless they had experienced it themselves.

Father Charlie was speechless when he came to pick me up at the hospital. They let me stay two nights. Then baby Kayla and I would be on our own. Father Charlie offered to drive us home to the Bronx.

I laid Kayla's going-home outfit on the bed. She was in the nursery so I could shower and get dressed. They only fed her water, since I was nursing. She latched on so quickly and drank her first mother's milk with gusto.

Still weak from delivery, I moved like an old lady. I sat in the shower on a bench and lingered as the warm water washed over my sore body. It felt good to be clean.

I pressed Kayla's little outfit with my hands. A tiny suit with violet flowers printed over soft white cotton. I had socks and a bonnet to match. So far, Kayla had lived clothing free, swaddled in a receiving blanket. The nurse taught me how to swaddle her, and I practiced it several times.

"I think someone wants her mommy," the nurse said as she brought Kayla back to me, cranky and crying.

"Ohh, baby, here I am," I said. The nurse put her in my arms. I stared at her round, pink face, still amazed at her beauty and uniqueness. I gazed into her eyes as she nursed. Sometimes she would gaze into my eyes, and other times she would close her eyes and suckle sweetly.

Kayla started to slow down and drift into that dazed, almost drunken state when she was full. I slipped my finger in the corner of her mouth, just like the nurses taught me, to break the suction and unlatch her mouth from my nipple.

The beauty of nursing amazed me. I was in awe of God's perfect design of a mother feeding her baby.

Father Charlie entered my room just as we were finishing and I was buttoning up. By the look on his face I don't think he had seen too many newborns. He was maybe thirty-two at the oldest, and even though he'd seen his nephew Ben this was still a new experience for him.

"Do you want to hold her?" I asked.

"She's so tiny," he said. He held her for a moment. Then we laid her on the bed, and he helped me put on her little outfit. "I can't get over how small she is."

"She's a healthy seven pounds, fourteen ounces," I announced.

"Wow, so that's what seven pounds looks like," he said.

Together we put her little arms through the armholes and her short legs in the bottoms. The outfit was labeled "newborn," but she was lost in the violets with extra material on both ends.

"What do you think?" I asked her. She just squirmed and cooed. I swaddled her in a new, white cotton blanket and laid her in her car seat. I strapped her in, and Father Charlie picked her up.

"You ready to go home, baby?" he asked.

"We're ready," I said in my little girl voice.

CHAPTER 33

Since my ride home from the hospital in Father Charlie's old blue Chevy I'd not been back out into the world. Michelle was visiting her sister, so my first week home it was just me and my new baby. Even though I felt a little unsure, it was nice to have the apartment to myself. Just the two of us, getting to know each other. In the hospital the nurses would tell me when it was time for a feeding and time to rest. They brought me my meals every four hours, and they helped me care for Kayla.

Now it was just me. No nurses, no meals, no help. Just me and this new little person they had entrusted into my care. I was solely responsible for this little life.

Kayla slept, making no sounds. She lay on her back, her head tilted to the side, her little fingers gripping her blanket. I just stared at her. Taking her all in. Admiring her round little face and chubby cheeks. Her fingers were so delicate and soft. Her lips were bright strawberry red and shaped like a rosebud. She had the longest eyelashes I'd ever seen. The little fuzz of hair she had was ruddy brown. Her eyes were still inky blue, and the whites of her eyes were light blue like the hospital scrubs. I couldn't keep my eyes off her.

I couldn't believe she was mine.

Friday, May 18. First home feeding: 30 minutes. That was my first entry in my blue stenographic notebook. I was careful to write down everything Kayla did. Every detail was recorded so I would be prepared for the next day. If only it was so simple and predictable.

The more I nursed, the more my milk came in. The funny thing was that I wasn't a milk drinker. I had never liked it. But the first two weeks I was home I craved it more than water. I easily drank a gallon a day. When friends would call to visit and ask, "Can I bring you anything?" I would ask them to bring me a gallon of milk. That little bundle of mine could drink. She'd nurse for about thirty minutes, fall asleep, and then two hours later would want more. She drained me dry.

The first few days my spiral notebook looked like this: Feeding; nap for two hours; eat again; bowel movement; lie there and look around; sleep, wake up and nurse again. I tried to alternate breasts like the nurse had said to help with the soreness. By the third day my nipples were red and chapped. I couldn't wear a bra or shirt. I'd have to air dry and coat with Vaseline. The nurse said that my nipples would toughen up and I'd get used to it, but that initial latch on took my breath away.

On day four I added a bath to the routine. I filled my white plastic tub with warm water and baby soap. The hospital gave me a gentle plastic brush. I held her head in one hand and cupped my other hand, ladling warm water on her small body and tender scalp. She kicked and squirmed and seemed to like it. I wrapped her in a yellow hooded towel when she was done and snuggled her close. No one warned me how good that would feel. It was more love than I had ever known. I held her tight to my chest, warming her shivering body.

On day five she stopped nursing for a few moments and stared into my eyes. She searched me and seemed to say, "So you are my mom." She had only known the inside of me and my voice. Now she was getting to know the outside. A lot to take in for such a small soul.

Sleep did not come easy some nights. She squeaked and squirmed until four in the morning. If she couldn't sleep then I couldn't sleep. My nights blended into my days. Between two and four in the morning were her fussy times. Sometimes nothing I did would console her, and she would just have to cry. It broke my heart to hear those cries.

Kayla loved her swing. When all else failed I would put her in the seat, wind it up, and watch her swing back and forth. I lay on the couch until she fell asleep, and then I would do the same.

By day ten of writing down her every move, including the color of her poop, I relaxed a little and put down the notebook. I no longer had to read Wednesday's entries to see what to do on Thursday. My God-given mothering instincts were kicking in. We had found our rhythm. We were mother and daughter, moving to our own music in the sweet dance of love.

CHAPTER 34

Today is Mother's Day. My baby is nine hundred miles away finishing her first year at college. This is the first Mother's Day in twenty years that we have not been together. It's a miracle she is even at Cornell College. I raised her by myself, but I was never alone. God stepped in as her Father. He provided more for my daughter than I could hope or imagine. My parents fell in love with their granddaughter the second they saw her. They gave her the same unconditional love as they gave me. They were a huge support as I raised her. My child was swimming in love.

I lay in bed, remembering all the past Mother's Days. Since she was five years old she made me breakfast in bed. Homemade blueberry muffins. A fried egg, orange juice. And when she got a little older she made me coffee. She insisted I eat the whole meal in bed. She carried in the feast on a silver tray, her curls bouncing around her face as she trotted into my room. A single flower was always in a vase. Often from our garden. And a handmade card. I loved the cards the best.

But today was different. I had no breakfast in bed. Rain rattled the plastic covering on the back patio. I listened, savoring the moment. A pink card had come in the mail the day before and was sitting on the dresser under the window. I was saving it for today.

I poured myself a cup of hot coffee, picked up the pink envelope, and slid back under my covers, pulling my quilt up to my chest.

With care I slid my thumb in the crease of the glue strip and opened the card. Different kinds of pink flowers adorned the front of the card. Behind the flowers was a picture of an open Bible. The store-printed verse began: "When God chose you as my mother. . .He chose the best mother for me." It was a sweet message. But I was hungry for the handwritten words written below in blue ink. And this is what my baby daughter wrote:

> You have set such an example of what it is for a woman of God to lead a life of strength, faith and beauty. I am growing into the woman I am today because of your influence and guidance. God chose you to be my mom for a reason. And I am so glad that you chose life for me— otherwise I would have never known *you.*
>
> I love you, Mom.
> Kayla

That chatty cabby back in New York had been right. I had all I needed.

ABOUT THE AUTHOR

A s a single mother, Bonnie Prestel knows the unique struggle and heartache of raising children alone. She is a graduate of Colorado State University and moved to New York city to begin her writing career. Bonnie worked for *WOMAN* magazine in Manhattan and has written articles for *Single Parent Family, The Denver Post, The Manitou Marque, The Catholic Herald, The Colorado Christian News* and many others. Bonnie was an editor at David C. Cook and also edited books for Andrew Wommack Ministries.

God blessed Bonnie with a husband at the age of fifty-two. Bonnie and Tim live in Colorado Springs and have four grown daughters. In her spare time, Bonnie enjoys gardening, reading, and cycling with her husband.

Connect with Bonnie.

To read more inspiring stories and words of encouragement, join Bonnie's private Facebook group or read her weekly blog. www.bonnieprestel.com.

To book Bonnie to speak at your women's event or retreat, complete the short questionnaire on her website.

Follow Bonnie on Twitter, LinkedIn, Facebook and Pinterest.

Printed in the USA
CPSIA information can be obtained
at www.ICGtesting.com
JSHW022332140824
68134JS00019B/1429